# FIND
# ME

## Also by Virginia Young

### By a Thread
A contemporary novel

### Out of the Blue:
A Massachusetts Romance

### The Birthday Gift:
A Connecticut Romance

### Sleepless Tides:
A Maine Romance

### Winter Waltz:
A Vermont Romance

### A Family of Strangers:
A Romantic Suspense

### I Call Your Name:
A Romantic Suspense set on
Martha's Vineyard

### Where Seagulls Sleep
A Romantic Suspense set in
Rhode Island

### Nocturnal
A Young Adult Novel

### Annasheeva
A Contemporary Novel

### Stone
A Contemporary Novel

# FIND ME

## A Collection of Short Stories

Virginia Young

*Riverhaven Books*
*www.RiverhavenBooks.com*

The stories contained within *Find Me* are works of fiction; any similarity regarding names, characters, or incidents is entirely coincidental.

Published in the United States by Riverhaven Books
www.RiverhavenBooks.com

ISBN: 978-1-937588-21-2

Printed in the United States of America
by Country Press, Lakeville, Massachusetts

Cover design and formatting by
Stephanie Blackman

*For Ed and Stephanie*
*with my deepest appreciation for their constant*
*encouragement and incredible help - without*
*them, my words would stay locked in the*
*darkness of a drawer, begging to see the light.*

*In memory of*
*Michael (Wolf) Pasakarnis,*
*June 25, 1981 - September 8, 2010.*
*"You are an unrepeatable onceness."*
*Karl Rahner, Jesuit*

# Table of Contents

# YOU CAN'T FIND ME

She stood at a makeshift easel and slashed shades and shapes of blue shard-like streaks and knife-blade gray paint across an oblong scrap of Masonite. With the surface completely covered, the finished piece closely resembled a turbulent, storm-filled evening sky. She breathed deeply, left the brush to soak in an old jelly jar half filled with tepid water, and felt her hands, her arms, her entire body relax.

Consumed, she sat down on the floor of the attic and scanned the painting, as if she'd just given birth. She liked it. She wasn't sure why, but the hues were blending, greeting one another easily, and for whatever reason the exertion from creating it had set her free, temporarily.

She lay back until she could feel her spine and shoulder blades against the hard wood floor and she stared at the dark, slatted ceiling. With her right arm bent to cover her eyes against the pure north light insisting itself through two ample windows, she closed her eyelids and felt drained, as if she'd participated in and won an intense physical fight.

After ten or twelve minutes, she sat up straight and stared again at the blue painting. It was, she knew, a reflection of her misery exposed.

Her eyes moved to the windows where deepening gray and fast-moving clouds assembled, and she could tell by the light that it was getting late. She needed to move from this space. She stood, collected the jar of water, and called to the cat. They needed to be downstairs. He'd soon be home.

# THE TRUNK

Decorated in faded gold against weary black, the small trunk begged to be bought, opened, discovered.

A magical piece, there was something appealing about its domed top and ornate brass hinge-work and clasp. If only there'd been a key.

Because the trunk was light in weight, the antique dealer, who had marked on its price tag *Lady's hat box*, was certain that, if there was something inside, it was paper, and not much of it. Rather than risk breaking the clasp, she sold the trunk at a reasonable price, unopened.

\*\*\*

Julia carried her new possession to the coffee table and sat down on the sofa to take a closer look. She leaned back, then sat forward and placed her hands at the sides where brittle leather straps threatened to shed bits of crisp skin or old paint.

She lifted the trunk then placed it down, turning it from side to side, examining the curved top and the flat bottom. How, she wondered, would she get it open without damage to the beautiful but keyless clasp? All hardware, the two hinges and the front lock, were apparently fastened from the inside. No sense trying to use a screwdriver to carefully remove the brass.

Frustrated, Julia stood up. Keeping her eyes on the object while walking towards the kitchen, she nearly stepped on the cat's tail. "Good God, Archie," she said, startled. "Trip me up why don't you?" Then with apologies, she lifted the huge orange cat and gave him a hug. "Okay," she said as she plopped him down in a chair, "I need caffeine. I need to think." The cat gave her a disinterested look, then hopped off the chair and walked into the living room.

Julia smiled and poured herself a generous mug of freshly brewed coffee. She took a sip then headed back to the trunk.

Archie had now placed himself on the coffee table next to the new attraction and proceeded to paw at one leather handle.

"Cut it out, Archie," she scolded. "If you wreck my new trunk, I'll swat your bottom." The cat blinked lazily and folded his innocent paws

2

back, half under his furry white chest.

"Bottom," she repeated the last of her warning softly. "Maybe the bottom."

Julia moved the coffee mug to the floor to make more room then tipped the trunk up on its dome. She could hear the paper, or something like paper, move inside — a fluttering-butterfly sound. The bottom of the trunk was a piece of wood, painted black; it measured about fourteen by eighteen inches. It was fastened in sixteen places along the four edges with worn black nails, their heads large enough to pry with perhaps a slim butter knife. Julia walked back to the kitchen and made a quick return to the sofa. A gulp of warm coffee, and then the painstaking procedure began. Metal against metal – she worked slowly in order not to harm the old wood. One by one. Over a period of more than an hour, Julia worked, the coffee growing cold, until the last nail was removed and carefully joined the others in a small pewter bowl.

Inserting the knife along one edge of the bottom, she pried the rectangle of wood, stubborn with age-hardened paint, until it could be moved.

"Wow," she exclaimed to the cat. "I did it!"

Now that she had access to the trunk, she hesitated.

"God," she said aloud, "I hope there isn't a dead spider in there or something." With one edge of the knife creating a wedge, she lifted the wooden panel and found that the interior, although faded with time, was lined in a beautiful print: cream with tiny pink roses and dainty trailing vines of pale green. Julia touched the rippled surface with one tentative finger. There were a few sheets of loose onionskin paper and one envelope, which felt light but occupied. Julia looked at the finely scrawled words in brown ink on its surface, *Fall River, Massachusetts*, a connection to the past. Someone cared enough about these papers to place them in a locked trunk.

Before settling down to read the small print, she maneuvered the clasp from the inside with the edge of her knife and it willingly popped open, as if it realized that all efforts to conceal the contents were now futile.

Julia tipped the trunk into an upright position and carefully lifted the domed top. She loved it. Someone else had loved it, too. That's what she found intriguing about antiques. They weren't just old, they were a part of history; significant or insignificant, a link with another

3

human being, who had probably hoped, dreamed, and loved.

She would read the words the trunk had long held captive, but first she placed the papers back inside, out of Archie's grasp. She warmed her coffee in the microwave then headed back to the sofa where she found herself hesitant to begin. It all seemed slightly intrusive, but, she decided, words were meant to be read.

Julia took a few sips of coffee then reached for the contents of her new find. Carefully, but with a determined hand, she opened the unsealed envelope and took from it a folded sheet of paper and an old photograph of a young woman.

In one hand she held the onionskin sheets, written in an obviously different style from the now unfolded paper. She glanced from one to the other, wondering which to read first. The folded sheet was dated July 19, 1860. The first of the onionskin sheets was dated July 19, 1878. She would read the oldest first, but before beginning, she took a few moments to study the profile of a young woman in a dark dress, her hair coiled away from an interesting but unremarkable face. The picture was dated on the back and held a singular name, Marisa – 1856.

The folded sheet was now unfolded and straightened: Julia began to read.

July 19, 1860
Fall River, Massachusetts


My Poor Christina,

It is with a heavy heart, but with great confidence that I have committed the acts of today. A turn of fate has placed me in a position to mimic God himself, and I pray he forgives me.

That I should, in my midwifery, serve two young women on this day, and that one should lose her child and one should lose her life, seems unfair and certainly cruel.

You, my dear Christina, must forever keep the secret, that, having delivered a fine baby girl to a mother who then died, I gave to you that child, to somehow replace your sweet baby boy, who died this day of his birth. The boy you will always hold dear in your heart will rest forever with poor, tormented Marisa.

Her mother and father put her through a living hell when they

4

discovered that she was unwed and with child. Just days ago, in a fit of rage, she bludgeoned her parents to death and attempted to end her own life as well. The attempt left poor Marisa irreparably broken, thus her death at the birth of her strong child.

Raise this girl, Christina, and give to her the love you longed to wrap around your son. Mourn, but not to take away from the breathing child in your care. No one but you and I will ever know her true identity.

God willing, she will bring you and your husband great joy. My deep sorrow to you in the tragic passing of your infant son.

Your nurse and friend,
Emma Ward

Julia sat, stunned with learning such a sad secret of babies switched. A baby boy buried with a stranger, a baby girl raised by someone she might never have known.

Julia studied the picture of Marisa. "Poor, tormented Marisa," the midwife had written. She placed the photograph and letter together in the trunk then began to read the other rippled sheets.

July 19, 1878

It is on this day I feel that I must share this burden with my girlhood trunk, and, perhaps someday, with someone who will persist in its opening. My intent is to bury the key to prevent an inquisitive girl from a discovery she need not know.

Julia shivered, rubbed her eyes, and read on.

Today is my dear daughter's celebration of birth. She is eighteen. She is solid and serene most times, but troubled, I fear. I pray it is not of my doing.

Over the years, I have often observed my child watching the preparation of a corpse for the grave. Her godfather's occupation, that of an undertaker, seems to have fascinated our child. When I have found her widened eyes viewing the very blood being drained away from stolen life, I have made myself known with a timid cough and then urged her away with some distraction. Surely, I have questioned myself at least one hundred times. Was I the best mother this child

5

could know? In losing my precious infant son, Andrew, I gained this motherless child. In her eighteenth year, I am aware that my health is poor and time is short. The great concern is what will become of my daughter?

My husband has shared more than an admiring glance at Clara, who disguises herself as my friend. I know deep in my heart that when I am no longer, it is Clara who will fill my shoes, my home, my bed. But what of my daughter, who senses all of this, I believe, and despises the woman who could become her stepmother?

It is at times such as this that I recall Marisa, who took the lives of her parents and ultimately her own. I pray fervently that God forgives the secret kept from all but the now-deceased midwife and myself. I pray that my daughter will accept changes without the rage that has threatened to surface when circumstances discouraged her plans.

I have tried and I have loved my daughter, to whom I gave the name, Lizzie Andrew.

Christina May Borden

(Published by Level Best Books, *Blood Moon*, 2012)

# LONGING

*You are my oxygen,* she thought each time she saw him, certain that without him, she would collapse and disintegrate like crepe paper in water. She could not, would not, suffer the absence of him for long. She would die without him, and it would all be over. It terrified her when she realized how much she loved him, and that's when she ran. It was nearly twelve years later when the call came from her brother.

"Come on, Madi," his voice begged. "Do this for me."

Madi sat down at the white marble-topped island in her kitchen over-looking Tilson Sands at Rhode Island's posh coastal stretch. She'd been fortunate finding and buying this quaint gardener's cottage. Small, with one bedroom and an open floor plan, she'd decorated with beautiful and useful antique chests of drawers and soft sofas and chairs in crimson against white-walled backdrops and colorful oriental rugs. It was a warm and comfortable common room. The charm of the place had captivated her, twelve-hundred miles from where she'd grown up, from where she'd left Simon. Now, with the phone pressed against her right ear, she walked into her living room space and sat down as her eyes scanned the workmanship, the post and beam structure with its wide plank floors, the mellow patina reminding her of melted butter, and the clear, leaded-glass windows that invited sunlight to display itself in diamond shapes of pure northern light.

"Are you there?" Robert asked when she'd given him no reply.

Madi sighed as quietly as she could manage and asked, "Why me?"

She thought about her brother, three years her senior. His best friend had been the love of her life, he just hadn't known it. She didn't think she could ever measure up to him. He was handsome, sweet, smart, and funny. Her thirteen-year-old heart was hooked from the moment his sixteen-year-old frame filled her parents' kitchen doorway for the first time. That depth of feeling didn't go away. She loved him for years, dating others in high school and college, always making the comparison. No one could be Simon.

"He needs a new start, Madi. I mean the guy has had it tough:

nineteen freaking months in Iraq, and for the second time. Be his friend, let him in. I know you always had a crush on him. Come on, I'm asking you to just kind of guide him. He's my best friend. If he'd stay here in Chicago, I'd watch over him, but I can't just leave my practice and follow him around. He wants Rhode Island, where he spent part of his childhood. He asked about you."

There was silence following his statement. "Madi?"

"I did not have a crush on Simon. Why did you say that?"

She could hear Robert sigh. "Okay, so no crush. But you liked him, everyone liked Simon. Help him out by just offering some friendship, Madi. Come on, give the guy a break."

"I had no idea Simon had ties here. When is he arriving? I'm busy as heck, you know that. Even though I work mostly from home, I have days I need to go in to Providence and Boston. I have things going on, Rob."

"I know that, Madi."

"Has he found a place to stay? I mean, he can't stay here, you know what I have for space."

"He found an efficiency unit. His allotment doesn't give him much. I offered him money, but you know him. He's proud. He's a smart guy, and I hope to hell he gets his life back, but they said it could be a long and bumpy road. He has those damn night tremors. Post-traumatic stress they call it. The guy's a hero, Madi. He's the best. Please."

Madi bent over in half, feeling nearly ill at the thought of letting Simon into her life again. It had taken years to purge the passion she'd felt for him and, although she had never quite succeeded, here she was, about to face the demons again, the love that was so strong it molded her into shapeless jelly. She pushed her shoulder-length auburn hair back from her tear-filled eyes and struggled with the words. "I'll give it a try, Rob, but I guarantee nothing. I'm not his therapist. I can offer him a cup of coffee here and there, and I can show him around Tilson, but other than that…"

"Fantastic," Robert said. "I knew you'd come through for us, Mad. I'm not asking you to do any more than befriend him. Give him some hope. So, is it okay for me to give him a call tonight with your address and phone number?"

Madi shivered and managed a weak "yes" before their conversation slid around to their parents and finally to an end.

With the phone in her hand, she straightened her back and walked to where a comfortable sofa waited. She sat down at one end, her eyes following the grey-white clouds floating over the sea. She was thirty and a successful analyst who found solace in painting soft seascapes in watercolor to fill the self-inflicted emptiness. Simon was thirty-three and a mess.

***

When he knocked on her door two days later, she stood for a few moments, almost breathless with anticipation. She was leaving for Boston to attend college when she'd seen him last. He was enjoying the party life of Chicago with her brother while attending Northwestern before entering the service. When she stepped forward and opened the door, she thought she might faint. He was more handsome than she had remembered: that dark hair, those green eyes, and his shoulders were broad. He didn't look ill in any way, and then he smiled.

"Holy smoke," he said as he appraised her from head to toes. "Who gave you permission to grow up so beautiful?"

Madi stepped back and he stepped inside.

"This is nice," he said as his eyes scanned the room. "It suits you."

Madi swallowed and wondered if her dry mouth could find words. She closed the door to chilled October wind and invited him to sit and asked would he have coffee. He accepted. With his hands in his trouser pockets, he walked slowly around the room taking in the details. Madi poured two mugs of coffee and handed one to him.

"You still take it black?" she asked.

Simon's mouth formed that familiar crooked little smile. "I can't believe you remembered. What's it been, twelve years? I'm impressed."

Madi sat down at one end of a sofa and found the strength to look directly into his wonderful eyes as he seated himself across from her. He'd been her romantic downfall, the boy she knew to be sought after by every girl in all the local towns. He was too handsome, too charming, completely divine, but so out of reach for a plain, skinny little teenager with long, straight hair and no particular abilities other than devouring book after book, absorbing the flowing prose with a fervor.

"I remember a lot," she said with just the slightest hint of a smile.

Simon shook his head, cradling the mug of hot coffee in his hands.

9

"Me too," he said. "You know, if you hadn't been Rob's sister, I'd have been all over you."

Madi squinted her eyes and then looked away from him before placing her coffee mug on the table next to her. "Simon, you had every girl in Chicago and surrounding towns after you — the star football player, the perfect dancer, the good student. Even my parents talked about what you were made of. You wouldn't have given me the time of day."

Simon looked at her as he sat forward. "I'm telling you, Madi, I had this thing for you. If you hadn't been Rob's little sister, oh yeah, I'd have been right there."

Madi sat very still for a few moments looking at his face for even a glimmer of a smile. He was serious, and she was silently amazed.

"So," Simon said, "Rob told you I live in town? It's not much, nothing like this, but at least I'm back. I missed the ocean in Chicago. This is the area where my grandparents lived, and so did I until I was twelve. It feels like home; I'm really glad to be here."

Madi nodded. "I understand. Listen, I go out of town on consultations sometimes. If you ever want to come here and just unwind, I'll give you a key. You can call, and if I don't answer, just come over. Make yourself some coffee, enjoy the view."

"You'd let me use your place? I'd love being able to come here. It's only about a two-mile walk. Thank you, Madi, I'm grateful for the invitation. And I accept."

"Did you walk here this evening?" she asked.

Simon took a swallow of coffee and nodded. "No car at this point. The doctors don't think I should be driving for a while. The feet work; it's okay."

Madi remembered that he'd had Corvettes, a red one, then a silver one, gifts from an indulgent father. "Well, if you come here and you feel too tired to walk back into town, these two sofas are comfortable. There are blankets in that chest of drawers by the door, so just make yourself at home."

After she'd said the words, she wondered if she'd offered too much. But he was walking, and if he came here at night, what would be the harm in his sleeping on a sofa? After all, this wasn't a stranger. This was Simon.

***

10

Madi opened her eyes, squinting against early morning light and noted that there was the feeling of warmth and weight across her side and waist. Simon. Simon had let himself in and sometime during the night slipped in beside her. She turned just enough to see his relaxed face so near to her hair. She thought about waking him and causing a fuss, scolding him for being there uninvited to her bed. She turned away, allowing the right side of her face to once again rest on her pillow, and then she smiled. She could scold him from now until forever, but he would not change, and she loved his being there, against her, always claiming to have slept better, without the troubling dreams, her at his side. Simon. And then she reminded herself that he was broken. It would not be fair, and maybe not real, to accept the relationship she longed for.

She deliberately moved slowly, slipping her bare legs from beneath the covers and pulling the satiny fabric of her nightshirt down over her knees. She would make coffee; he would want that black brew first thing. As she started to stand, his hand reached out for hers.

"Hey," she said, "let go."

He pulled her back into the supple lavender scented sheets, hugging her close to him.

"Let go," she said. "And what are you doing here anyway? Really Simon, you're like a stray cat. I never know when you're going to show up."

He smiled and closed his beautiful eyes for just a moment.

"I've wondered more than a few times over the last few months about my logic in having given you a key. I think it might be time for you to forfeit that."

He unwillingly let go of her hand and shifted himself up against a pillow, his sage green t-shirt revealing lean, muscled arms. "You'd make me give up the key? I still get those headaches. This is the only place I sleep without waking in misery. You wouldn't really take my key away, would you?" He smiled, and at the same time gave her a pleading look.

"Oh yes, I would," she said, and then she moved away toward the bathroom. In the privacy of that small room, she looked into the mirror and smoothed back her hair, brushed her teeth and gently rubbed her face and neck with a warm, damp cloth and a touch of almond soap. Having completed that brief motion, she looked at her eyes and knew

11

that it would take almost nothing to flood them with tears. Simon, he was so forbidden to her; more unattainable than ever in his vulnerable condition.

In the kitchen where she scooped coffee into a French press, he watched her as he lazily leaned against the white, marble-topped island in the center of the room.

Madi refused to acknowledge his presence, but she thought back to a few nights ago when he'd knocked on her door after eight and joined her once again in watching an old movie. His hand had rested, almost singeing the skin on her bare knee, and she'd deliberately moved away, standing and walking to the kitchen from where she'd offered coffee.

"Are you sorry to know me, Mad?" He interrupted her thoughts. "Do you want me to go?"

She turned for just a moment and glanced at him. He looked saddened and she sighed before turning back toward the stove. "Come on, Simon. I'm not sorry to know you, not at all sorry if I've helped you in any way, but having you climb into my bed is another issue. I told you that the sofa was yours when you need it. I never invited you to crawl in bed beside me."

He smiled as he poured himself a cup of coffee. "But we fit so well together. I love sleeping next to you."

Madi gave him a stern glance. "That's not in my guide book on friendships with people who have issues with nightmares and headaches. For God's sake, Simon, I'm a therapist, but not yours, and it's a good thing too. I mean," she said with a spatula and two eggs in her hands, "what do you suppose people would think if they knew you slept with me? *Slept* with me. That has a connotation of its own. People would never believe we just sleep."

"When did you become so concerned about what others think?" he asked as he ran his fingers through thick hair. "You push me away, Madi. I'd be here with you every night if you'd let me; you must know that. When I stay away, it's to give you a break from me."

Madi turned away from him toward the stove. She didn't want a break from him. She was about to crack the eggs into a pan when she noticed him walking back toward the bedroom, leaving his nearly full cup of coffee on the otherwise empty island, as if it was the one important thing in the room. She closed her eyes and then opened them again as she slipped the eggs back into their carton. Simon, she thought,

12

I cannot injure you. I'm supposed to help mend you. Simon.

She waited a few minutes then walked toward the bedroom where she would try to explain, maybe at last to empty her heart and tell him the truth, but he was gone. She sat down on the edge of the bed and pressed her left palm against the pillow where he had slept.

***

Weeks passed by and she did not see him. She changed the sheets and her own pillow case several times, leaving his as it was, where she could close her eyes at night to touching where he had been, and where she would open her eyes in the morning to see the empty space.

# CHRISTMAS EVE

It was that time of day when light trades places. The trees became black sketches against a blue-gray sky, while candles and dimmed lights inside lay golden warmth upon familiar things.

John sat in his old crimson chair, a cup of cooled coffee on a little round table to his right. He blinked his faded blue eyes and smiled at the one-foot-high Christmas tree with ten perfect little white lights begging for his approval. Dear Mary had put that little tree together just a year before she passed away, with only one-inch white paper stars for decorations that she had cut and lovingly fastened in place. Their other decorations, all the memories of their Christmases together and with the children, had been packed off to family, friends, and a charity in the hopes of easing the pain of losing a second son. It was years later that Mary decided that they once again needed the spirit and light of a little tree. How does one manage to go on, he wondered, without your beloved companion of more than sixty years? He missed Mary terribly; this would be his third year without her.

He looked at the pictures on the wall near the stairway. There were two pensive faces looking straight ahead at a camera, the wedding day he so cherished. Mary, with her crown of white roses nestled in her glorious red hair, looked like a fairy princess in the simple white gown her grandmother had sewn for her. Two sons in uniform also graced those walls, both gone, one to an accident and the other to war; how beautiful they were, and how hideous that he and Mary would see them in the ground. It was intensely wrong, he believed, to bury your children. And Saffron, their wonderful Irish Setter, his picture was hung on that wall too, next to photos of three persnickety cats, Edgar, Tiger, and Fuzzy. It was a wall so loaded with the weight of love; you'd think it would just fall over.

John closed his moist eyes and slept. Early morning greeted him as he squinted into the pale gray sky and saw the subtle movement outside: snowflakes, large, twirling snowflakes, and tiny darting birds at the sill.

John stood and walked to the tin box under the window, raised the lower half of the glass, and placed a large measure of birdseed on the cold, narrow granite ledge. He closed the window and stood back, nodding as little feathers fluttered, grateful for their Christmas breakfast and the puffs of warm air from the window, which should have been repaired or replaced long ago.

He looked down and noticed his usually sparkling wood floor now smudged with bits of gray-black, a trail of soot coming from the chimney. And then he saw the three boxes at the foot of the table where the small tree stood and a scratchy note, 'Sorry for the mess.'

John held the note for a moment then picked up the three small containers. The first was wrapped in red and had been tied with a bright green bow. He did not hesitate; he was excited to have presents. John untied the bow and pulled at the glossy red paper. Inside, he found a word, printed in large letters, and a news article about the shaking of hands and melding of hearts throughout the world. The word was PEACE. John shook his head and smiled.

The second box was covered in gold paper, its bow a beautiful cobalt blue. Again, John eagerly untied the bow and pulled at the paper. With the box open, he pushed the tissue aside and found another word, and an official looking message, a cure had been found for cancer. Cancer had taken Mary. John smiled again and looked at the word, HOPE.

What fine gifts, he thought as he reflected on the past and allowed his eyes to enjoy the tiny tree and the softly falling snow.

The third package sat next to the original note on his lap. He read it again, 'Sorry for the mess.' It was a box sheathed in white paper tied with a big red bow. John was careful not to pull too hard on that ribbon, it was such a pretty thing and maybe he could drape it over something in the room later. He pulled at the paper then lifted the cover from the third box. Inside, he found only one word, LOVE, again, in large print. But it didn't matter that there was no other message, for immediately, his eyes went to those treasured photos on the stairway wall.

John sat back in his chair and folded his shaky hands in his lap. What very fine gifts, he thought, and then he smiled and closed his eyes.

# THE TRIP

Emma Weid didn't trust anyone. As the younger sister to a pair of terrible twin brothers, she often heard, "The boys will only want you for one thing." It took years, into her late teens, for Emma to realize what that "one thing" was.

When she met Eldon Weid at college, she found him attractive, but suspect. What did he really want from her? Her math skills? Her top-of-the-grade essays? Her petite and curvaceous body topped with a glorious head of curly auburn hair? She wasn't sure, but when he proposed, she said yes. And then when their two children, Charles and Christine were born, she cringed when the occasional person would remark that the children were growing like weeds, which was, of course, how their last name was pronounced.

Now, after a successful forty-year career as head mistress in a private school for girls, surviving widowhood from the age of seventy-one, Emma found that at the age of eighty-two her children were ready to see her settle into a facility where her needs could be properly met. She'd tripped and broken her right leg and ankle, which apparently meant that she had also broken her brain.

"Mother," Christine said, "I think you'll enjoy Willow Brook. There's absolutely no sense in you going back to your house after rehab. I can arrange to move you directly from here to your nice new quarters. Living as far from you as we do, it's quite a worry for us, you know, to be wondering if you're on the floor or something."

Emma looked at her stern fifty-four-year-old daughter. Christine was president of the Charlestown-Patriot Savings Bank and her husband was an investment banker. Their thirty-year-old son had just started his own software company in the heart of New York City. How, Emma wondered, did she grow old enough to claim a thirty-year-old grandson?

Emma hated arguing with Christine who never learned how to call it quits. To keep peace, Emma nodded her approval at her daughter's distasteful suggestion.

16

"Willow Brook sounds like a fine place," Emma lied. "I will, however," she continued with her most firm of voices, "go back home first. I will not go anywhere else directly from this hospital. I have things to address."

Christine sighed and looked frustrated. In her world, things were black and white, digits and dashes. "But you'll go soon?" she said. "Really, Mother, Charles and I are in agreement; this is the best solution."

Solution? Problems have solutions. They obviously considered her a problem.

Back at the place she'd called home for more than forty-five years, Emma assured Christine that she'd be fine on her own. Using a three-pronged cane issued to her by the rehab center, which she didn't need, she appeared to be both cooperative and capable for the time being. When the door closed behind her daughter, Emma made a face and a grunting sound indicating that she just might have her own ideas for the future.

Her attractive brick house on Storrow Drive in Boston was long ago paid for; money was not an issue. Emma looked out at the length of narrow, stone fenced backyard from her dining room's French doors. Eldon and she had enjoyed many an evening out there with their various dogs and one cat who'd invited himself in for at least a dozen years before he died three days after Eldon. Emma smiled recalling the good times. She liked it here, although it was large and sometimes lonely. She was ready for a small, and perhaps, temporary change.

She made a few phone calls and checked on her passport, which was up to date from a previous trip to Ireland. Christine just might wonder about that and check to see that everything was valid. Then she called a taxi to take her to a shopping mall about a mile from her home. The English Ford that sat in the garage was fine, but she wasn't all that sure about driving yet, that ankle was still a bit stiff. Besides, at eighty-two, maybe she'd let go of the driving. You hear so often about those batty old things putting a foot on the accelerator instead of the brake as they go flying into some place where they have no business being. Yes, she would give up the car, but quite definitely not the house. And as for Willow Brook, not now, not ever.

Back from her excursion by taxi, Emma tried on some of her new purchases and smiled at her reflection in the hallway mirror. She made herself a cup of Earl Grey tea then sat down to write Christine a note, which she would mail immediately.

Dear Christine,

    I know you believe that your plans for me are the right ones, but since I disagree, this is what I plan to do. I have made arrangements for the house to be monitored on a regular basis by someone I trust as much as myself. I will be away. When I return, and at this point, there is no schedule, I intend to sell the car. I've always intended to see the pyramids and Casablanca as well as some other exotic places. I'm going. Please don't look for me. I'm fine, in fact, never better. I'll tell you all about my adventures when I return.

Fondly,
Mother

    Emma packed her new clothes, stuffed an ample amount of cash into her purse, then called a taxi, which she took to Logan Airport. She found an empty stall in a ladies' room there where she made a few adjustments, and then she took another taxi back to the small apartment building directly across the street from her own house. She looked at the FOR-RENT sign in the second-floor window.

    Carrying her two light suitcases, wearing lime green tights and black sensible shoes, a black dress and coat and a generous full blonde wig, which she cheerfully referred to as her "escape roots," she walked to the building's door.

    From the large picture window in her spacious yet sparsely furnished new digs, Emma smiled as she held a small bottle of ginger ale to her brightly painted lips. "See you later this evening, dear house," she said aloud, watching sparrows dart amidst her eaves. Then she took another swig.

# THE WEIGHT OF SNOW

Meg stood in the 1930's-style kitchen of the old farmhouse, which had once been the home of her grandparents. They'd died there, both of them in their eighties, grateful that they'd never had to go to a nursing home as some of their friends had. Her father, their only child, had moved in with them and took care of the small farm and the needs of his parents, even to feeding them spoons full of pureed food and warm soup. Now, four years after they'd passed on, so did her father at a premature stage in his life. It was her turn, not to take care of the humans – because none were left – but to take care of the animals and to decide their fate and that of the quaint farm just outside of Manchester, New Hampshire.

She looked out through the window over the kitchen sink. From the light on the back porch, she could see that the snow was determined to cover everything outside – to proclaim itself as the prominent part of the night and the typical Northern New England blizzard. Meg leaned closer to the window, the sink's edge against her hipbones; she could see a dim light from the one barn window that faced the back of the house. It was an old barn, small, in need of repair. Milo was in there with Jake, probably both of them cold.

Meg pulled on a pair of clumsy boots and took a scarf that smelled of charred wood from the coat rack and wound it around her neck. She slipped her arms into a navy-blue coat and fastened only two buttons, then carelessly plopped a cranberry-colored tam on her head to protect her hair from the wet snow. With a flashlight in her gloved hands, she opened the kitchen door, gusts of snow-filled wind allowing itself in as she stepped out into the cold, her eyes squinting against the abrasive, biting squall. With the flashlight's full beam to guide her, she walked, taking high steps through eighteen-inch snow, forty yards to the barn. There, with the flashlight tucked tightly between her knees, she used both hands to unlatch and pull open the heavy barn doors tethered by a deep drift of white. Milo turned to look at her with a low woof, lying down in the hay next to his friend, Jake, an old pinto who had been on the farm for all of Meg's twenty-eight years. The gentle horse had his back to her, but he turned his head to look toward her. Even with a blanket across his back, he looked cold, and Milo had a quiver to his ample white and butterscotch body. The dim light bulb hanging from a frayed wire on one of the rafters swayed slightly, indicating that wind was getting in. Meg directed the flashlight up and feared the place was not secure. It was all on her now. What could she do with this old horse and his dog friend who would not leave him? They weren't safe, and they certainly weren't warm, in this frail old structure.

She looked around at this place where once she had loved to play, and found reins, halter, and saddle against the wall next to the door. She looped the halter over Jake's head, who didn't seem to mind. Milo stood, ready to go wherever Jake was going. Meg led the horse to the door, Milo at his side, and managed to get the three of them all outside before raging wind slammed against the doors. She moved the latch in place then talked to the animals as she led them toward the house and to the kitchen door, which she opened. "Come on," she urged the reluctant horse, and then Milo entered the kitchen as if to tell the horse that it was all okay. It took a few tugs and gentle but firm words to get the creature inside, but once there, he looked around and Milo sank down onto the small rug in front of the sink. "Wonder what Dad, Gram, and Gramps would say to a horse in their kitchen," she said to the dog who acted like all of this was perfectly normal.

Meg kicked off the weighty boots and removed her jacket, hat, scarf, and gloves then wondered what to do next. The horse looked uneasy, but with side-glances here and there, Meg felt that he knew his options were limited and he was still. She moved her moist jacket and boots, leaving them to dry on a small stack of newspapers on a chair by the stove. Then she pushed at the kitchen table in the center of the room until she had it away from the horse, giving him more room to move. She carried each of the four chairs to the table area, then removed Jake's halter. She told both of the animals that it would be fine as she went in search of blankets to place on the floor. She found an old rug rolled up and tied with rope in the storage room off the kitchen and decided that would be the best bet for Jake to stand or lay on. Dragging the heavy article into the kitchen, she used a serrated bread knife to sever the ropes and unrolled a worn but pretty Persian-style carpet, creating an eight by ten-foot area over the linoleum floor. "There," she said. "Now for a bucket and bowl of water to get you two guys through until morning." That done, she stood back and smiled. She wondered what her colleagues at the university would think of her now. Assessing the situation further, she placed a few newspapers on the floor at Jake's hind legs, just in case.

When the telephone rang, it alarmed all three of them. Milo gave a soft, wide-eyed woof and the horse's ears flicked to and fro. "Hello?" Meg answered.

"Megs," he said, "it's Glen. How're things going up there? I tried to get a flight out of Logan, but Boston's getting pummeled with snow. I might have to drive."

Meg shifted from one foot to the other then sat down. "Don't, Glen. It's a bad storm, there's no sense."

"You've got to be kidding. Of course, there's sense. You're there and I'm here."

"But you hate driving in this weather. It's late and it's slippery out there." She didn't add that there was also a dog and a horse in her kitchen, which she didn't think would go over well with him.

"I know, but I'll give it a try. I keep thinking about you alone up there, I remember how desolate that farm was when we visited your dad last year. Fields and forest, that's about it."

Meg closed her eyes and bit softly at her lower lip. She hated the way he mutilated her name by calling her Megs and Megsie, as if Meg wasn't good enough. The farm was more than fields and forest to her. It was isolated and could be lonely, but that was secondary to needs. She didn't think she'd be there at all if it weren't for Milo and Jake. She could try to find them a home, but who would take an old dog and a very old horse? Keeping them together was important. The situation was impossible.

"You'll just make me anxious, Glen. Don't come."

"I'll see what happens," he said. "I'm losing the signal here. I'll talk to you later."

Meg held the phone in her hand and looked at it, then placed it back on its receiver. Even if he decided to make the drive up from Boston, in this weather it could easily be twice the time, three, maybe four hours. She hoped he wouldn't make the attempt. It was after eight and the snow kept coming. She wondered too what she would find to talk with him about once he arrived. She'd tried many times to explain her

21

feelings, that he was a friend, nothing more. Glen acted as though her words had no impact. She thought about letting people into one's life. Often, it wasn't so simple getting them out.

Meg dimmed the kitchen light with a switch her electrician father had installed years ago, leaving the room and animals in semi-darkness. "You two behave," she said. "No parties."

In the small living room, she placed two more logs on the fire and drew one of her grandmother's old sweaters over her shoulders. The house creaked and moaned with the wind, and she worried about the roof. Before she sat down on the sofa, she decided to turn off a lamp by a window. As she did, she glanced out at the snow at the front of the house. She thought at first that it was a reflection she saw, and she strained her eyes to see it again, the light, a small light in the distance, like a flashlight in someone's hand. Instinctively, she moved back a foot or two, frightened about who would be out there in that forest; it seemed they were coming her way. Meg felt a surge of adrenalin. She looked around. What did she have for protection? She went to the phone and made a call to the police. She heard a recording that due to the weather the entire force was out on the roads. If there was an emergency, the caller could put in a request from the state police. Meg closed her eyes and held the phone for a moment before placing it back down. She didn't think she should disturb the state police for seeing a flashlight in the distance. Or should she? She went back to the window in the room lit only by the hearth's glow. She could no longer see a light. Where did it go? As she turned to walk toward the sofa, she saw the light again, but just for a moment. She stood there, almost hiding behind the curtains and drapes then decided to sit down.

It occurred to Meg that taking care of the farm and its four-legged inhabitants had been more of an undertaking than she had imagined. It stressed and saddened her to think of what she could do to make things right. Pulling a colorful afghan over her knees, she thought again of Glen. He was trying hard to be what she wanted, and just now, his presence wouldn't have been so bad. She thought about love, about how feelings didn't always line up, two people loving the same way at the same time, out of sync. Sorry that she didn't care for Glen in the way he cared for her, she closed her eyes and hoped he wasn't traveling the highways to be with her.

During the night, she reluctantly found small increments of light

22

sleep, only to be awakened by sounds, maybe a knock at the door, she wasn't sure. Each time, she listened, then tugged at the afghan and tried to relax.

When morning came, snow was still falling lightly; sun painted everything outside a subtle tinge of pink. She walked into the kitchen and found the pinto standing in the middle of the rug, looking bewildered. The dog was sitting just two feet away, still on the scatter rug near the sink. Meg spoke to the two creatures then looked out to the barn. Some of the snow had blown off the roof, but there were areas where it was deep, and that worried her. By daylight, she could get the small woodstove in there burning to warm up the place, but if the roof caved in, what good would that be? With boots on her feet and her jacket on, Meg walked to the barn to bring a pail of oats in for Jake. With a large mixing bowl filled, she offered it to the horse who was hesitant before lowering his head for the food. Milo had a can of dog food and later shared a slice of toast with Meg. As she swallowed a sip of hot coffee, the phone rang and she thought surely it would be Glen.

"Miss Harlow? Meg?"

"Yes," she replied, "is that you, Tom?"

"Sure is; just checking on you. Our caller system had your number on it from last night," the police chief explained. "Everything all right up there?"

"I think so. I happened to look out the window around eight and saw a light, like a flashlight, out near the woods. It spooked me a bit."

"Really? Strange to have someone out prowling around in the storm. We'll take a look in a little while and then we'll stop by. Anything we can bring to you? How are you set for wood?"

"I've got plenty, thanks. Dad had the back room filled with nice dry oak and some cherry."

"He was a good man, your father. Okay, someone from the department, maybe me, will stop by shortly to see how you're doing. Stay warm."

"I will," she said and placed the phone back on its perch. Then she wondered how she'd explain a horse and his dog in her kitchen. Maybe it would be in violation of a health department regulation. When she sat down again to finish her coffee, Meg thought about the farm. By daylight, it was a picture, but there was no doubt that repairs were needed. The university had been lenient with her, giving her as much

23

time as she needed to square things away. With her position as a curriculum planner, they'd told her that if needed, she could attend meetings once each week and do the rest of the work on her computer at home. Maybe that was the option she'd choose, keep the connection to Boston, drift gently away from Glen, and properly take care of this old farm, which now belonged to her. It could work for at least a while, giving Jake and Milo their last years in their rightful home. That was it; she'd stay and get the place in sound shape the way it had been when she was a child.

The knock startled her. She walked to the door where she could see a police cruiser and felt relieved.

"Tom, nice to see you. How're the roads out there?" she asked at the open door.

"Good, they're good now. All the plows and sanders are out; we're equipped for this stuff up here. Just wondered if I could talk to you for a minute."

"Oh, sure, come on in. I have a fresh pot of coffee, would you like a cup?"

"No, thanks though. I've been pouring it down my throat all night to stay alert."

"Okay, well, come in and sit down, Tom."

The fifty-something-year-old officer removed his hat and sat down in a chair across from where Meg sat on the sofa. "We had kind of a weird occurrence we discovered this morning. I'm thinking it must have been that incident with the flashlight you told me about."

Meg sat up straight. "What sort of occurrence?"

Tom looked down at the hat in his hands then back up to Meg's pretty face. "I'm afraid we found a body out there. Found a car that had been pulled off the road, like it was being concealed in the pines. Then we followed indentations in the snow and found this man, a flashlight in his right hand. A tree limb, loaded up with the white stuff, fell right on him. Can't figure out what he was doing out there in this weather. It doesn't make sense."

Meg took a deep breath. "Could it have been a hunter? Dad posted all sixty acres of land, but sometimes they claim they don't see the signs."

Tom shook his head. "I don't think so. This guy had a gun all right, but not a hunting type. It was a fancy little pistol he had in his coat

24

pocket. The license plate is from Massachusetts. ID states he's a fellow named G.J. Whitten. I'm trying to get some info on him now."

Meg felt stunned. Glen. What was he doing there around eight o'clock last night when he'd told her he was still in Boston?

"Are you all right? You look a little pale."

"I'm okay," she said slowly and softly. Then she looked at Tom. "I knew him. He'd planned to come up here later." She thought about what she didn't want to imply, that Glen had lied to her about where he was. She told Tom that Glen had family, a mother and sister in White Plains, New York. "His sister's married name is Buckley; I don't know the address," she added in a state of shock and confusion.

"I'm sorry," he said. "This must come as a terrible blow to you. The information you've given me will be a great help. Are you sure you're all right? Was this man someone special?"

"I'm okay," Meg answered in a half whisper, not okay at all. *Why had Glen lied concerning his whereabouts? Why the pistol?*

Tom stood and, when he did, he noticed the horse and dog in the kitchen. He placed his hat on his head and chuckled. "I see you brought old Jake inside."

"The barn is a wreck," she said. "I'm going to clean out the shed where Dad stored the farm equipment and put Jake and Milo in there until I can get the barn repaired. There's a little heat in there too, electric, enough to keep them comfortable."

Tom nodded and smiled as he moved toward the door. Meg shivered and pulled the old sweater closer to her throat.

25

# CIRCLE

The non-committing gray of the fog and morning mist entered her room without invitation.

Maura slipped out of bed, into the bathroom, out of the bathroom, then back into bed. She pulled the covers up to her chin, then threw them off and swung her slim legs onto the floor. She ignored the waiting slippers and walked with bare feet on the chilled oak floors to the cold marble squares in the kitchen.

On the back of a kitchen chair, she found the gray sweater and shoved her arms into its sleeves, pulling the worn garment close across her thin nightgown. It was all so cold: the day, the place, the task.

Someplace she'd read that life was like a circle, and that it was often hard to know the beginning and the end. Somehow, she did not relate this time to the *beginning* of anything.

Maura put a filter in the coffee maker, six heaping measures of coffee into the filter, filled the maker's container with cold water, and flipped the switch. She stood back, almost as if she'd just given birth and was watching her baby gurgle and hiss. It was energized, making coffee, it was doing more than *she* was.

Her feet were cold; she walked back to the bedroom and climbed into bed once more, the covers over just her feet. She glanced toward the window on her right where she could usually see the George Washington Bridge, but instead she saw only a dismal future.

*I've done this,* she thought, and then she said it out loud as if to make it more true.

I told him to go. I couldn't take it anymore, his awful absence from us, his apathetic "I don't care" and his "whatever you want," and then the jacket that arrived as a gift invading our home.

Maura slipped her feet from beneath the covers and threw Peter's sweater to the floor; she stepped over it as if it was a dead body and walked to her closet.

She chose a suit of navy blue and from her jewelry chest her garnet ring where once a gold band had been placed with a promise. She slid

26

her feet into her navy-blue pumps as she stared at the phone, allowing it to interrupt her miserable thoughts. She could hear herself answer, *Yes?* And she could hear him speak her name, the way he used to when they were dating, *Maura?* But she was on the other side of the room from the silent phone, aware that she was awake, yet dreaming, wishing.

She shook her head briefly; the courthouse wasn't so far away and it would all be over soon. Maura took her purse from the table in the hall. With *his* keys in her hand, she turned and looked at the furniture-filled empty room.

## DATING JOY

She sat at a card table on a folding chair next to an open window in her first-floor apartment. She had gleaming hardwood floors and almost no furniture because she knew what she wanted and simply couldn't afford it yet.

She worked intently, shoving her long, straight dark hair behind her left ear. With small steel prongs and flat-ended tools, using both of her hands, pushing here and pulling there, she persuaded the clay into a perfect little goat, horns and all.

The answering machine clicked on after a few annoying rings and she heard the voice of her friend.

"Hey, Juniper Joy, what are you doing? Pick up, Joy. Come on, I know you're there."

Joy hissed, threw a damp cloth over her goat and walked to the phone a few feet away. There was no chair there, so she sat down, cross-legged, on the shiny floor.

"What, Leah? I'm in the middle of a goat."

"A what?"

"A goat – clay. Anyway, what's up?"

"I want you to come out and play tonight."

"No, I can't. I'm busy."

"Are you kidding? No pun intended, but are you serious? Working on a goat?"

Joy moved the phone to her other ear. "I enjoy it, Leah. Remember? I seem to recall you begging for the polar bear I made last week. Besides, I need to do this, it's my therapy and I can use the money too."

Leah sighed. "I know, really. But all work and no play…"

"It's play to me."

"You need to come out tonight. Come on, we'll have a beer; that's affordable, and we'll have a good time. A little honky-tonk music, a few laughs. Talk about therapy!"

Joy looked at her watch. "What time are you thinking?"

"Around eight."

28

"It's seven-fifteen. I'm a mess. I can't make it by eight. Where are you going anyway? Bubba's?"

"Oh stop. What's Bubba's? We'll go to our usual, The Pitfall. Come on, Mike said he'd meet us there and he might bring a friend."

"Oh no you don't! I'm not getting set up again! No. No way. I'm staying home with my five-inch goat."

She could hear Leah's deep breath and imagine her friend's exasperation and the rolling of her eyes.

"Come on, Joy. We'll have fun. Take a shower and meet me there at eight. Okay, eight-thirty. Come on; you're becoming an introvert. It's not healthy."

"Are you really talking to me about health? Let me see. You eat burgers and fries. I eat apples and tofu." Again, Joy could envision her best friend making a scrunched-up face to tolerate the light-hearted truth.

"I know. But you're in need of social graces. Come on; go get ready."

Joy scrambled to her feet and tugged at her sleeveless white blouse, smoothing her sage green shorts. "What are you wearing?"

"Jeans and my new pink top. But wear whatever makes you happy."

"I'm happy nude."

Leah laughed. "I don't care; come naked if you want to. It'll sure liven up the place."

"I'll figure out something to wear," Joy said. "But who's this dude Mike might bring? I'm not in the mood for that kind of torture, Leah, I mean it. That last guy, Norman, what a creep! He never took his cowboy hat or leather gloves off all night. I still think he was hiding a fungus."

Leah giggled. "We all thought Norman was hiding a fungus, or something. No more Normans," she said. "I promise."

"Yeah, but does Mike promise? That's what I want to know."

"Yes," Leah said. "We both promise, really."

Joy took a shower and used the juice from real lemons in her hair. She dressed in an ankle-length brown skirt with orange flecks in the fabric and a sleeveless burnt umber blouse. Dark sandals, made from a synthetic material, no leather for her, cradled her slender feet. With tiny golden acorn earrings fastened in place, she brushed her long hair and decided that she was ready.

29

When she arrived at The Pitfall, Leah and Mike were sitting at the bar laughing, surrounded by three others, also laughing. There was Patti, a girl Joy couldn't stand and doubted that she had gone beyond third grade. She was with Gary, her long-time beau. Then there was a large, blond-haired man with a mouthful of the biggest, whitest teeth she had ever seen, except for that visit to the aquarium when she studied the sharks. She nearly turned to leave.

"Juniper Joy!" Leah called to her. "Come on over. Meet Bif."

Bif reached out to grasp and shake Joy's hand. Apparently, he didn't know that it should be the woman's option to shake or not to shake. "Mike told me all about you," he said with a broad smile.

Joy half smiled and nodded. She was definitely killing Mike. "I'll have a cold one," she said to the bartender.

"I'll get that for you," Bif said with his luminous smile.

"No," Joy said, "I'm all set." This guy, she thought, might assume he owned her for the night if he paid for her beer. "Thanks anyway."

"Let's get a table where we can all sit and be comfy," Leah said as they moved to a darkened circle of wood in the corner.

"So," Bif began as he pulled out a chair for Joy, "I heard you're a librarian. Does that mean we have to whisper?" he asked in a soft proud-of-himself voice, and then he laughed.

Joy shuddered inside and gave him a quick smile with closed lips. "Good one," she said and wondered how many more times she would be asked that question.

Bif's eyes grew almost brighter than his teeth. "I'm impressed. No librarian I ever knew looked like you. Boy, I just might start checking out some books."

And if only, she thought, you could do more than tear off the covers and eat the pages.

Leah and Mike, Patti, and Gary all watched the pair and listened through the loud music. At one point, Patti leaned toward Leah and Joy could half-hear and half-lip-read the words from Patti's red lips. "Cool, it looks like we made a match with Joy and Bif."

Leah smiled, took a sip of her beer and then folded her hands tightly into one impenetrable knot.

\*\*\*

Three weeks later, with her window open to the crisp early autumn air, Joy fashioned an eight-inch horse with her clay, adding an intricate braided mane. The phone rang and she let the answering machine do what she'd intended it to do.

"Juniper," came Leah's sweet voice, "it's a gorgeous evening, the sun's going down, let's go out. Pick up, Joy. Come on."

Joy scooted her folding chair back carefully so that she wouldn't scratch the beautiful floors. She loved her landlords; they were like the best ever grandparents, and they loved her as well.

"What now? Attila the Hun came back from the grave and needs a woman?"

Leah laughed. "Oh, come on. Bif wasn't that bad, was he?"

Joy rolled her eyes. "Worse."

"Look, it's not like I think you're needy or anything, but it's fun to have someone in your life. I hadn't met Bif before or I'd have known he wasn't your type. Sorry. But listen, let's just go for a walk and we can end up at The Pitfall for a beer or just some coffee. Come on, I need to walk in this terrific fall air."

Joy looked at her open window. The evening was beautiful, and she would love the walk. "All right, a walk and coffee, that's it. You won't have some weirdo lurking in the corner?"

"No weirdoes."

After an hour of chatting as they walked around their small town, they ended up at The Pitfall where they both ordered beer, thirsty from their fast-paced endeavor.

"Okay," Leah said as they moved to a small, intimate table away from the jukebox, "I need to talk to you about something and I don't want you to get all upset."

Joy squinted as she focused her attention on Leah. Now what, she wondered.

"Don't look at me that way," Leah begged.

"Okay. Don't fix me up with anymore of the limp and ludicrous from your lonely list."

Leah sighed and looked around the room, then back at Joy who was gulping down her beer.

"Look," Leah said, "I know we haven't found a good match for you yet, and I also know that you don't really need any help, but I need you to do me this one favor."

"I'm not for rent."

"I'm not renting you. Come on, Juniper, do me a favor. Please, I'm

31

desperate."

Joy placed her empty glass down on the table. "Desperate about what? Explain."

Leah put her half-full glass down and then folded her arms on the table as she leaned forward. "There's this guy, Brian. He's twenty-eight, has a great accounting job with the state. He's dying to meet you and maybe go out with you."

Joy looked at her friend. "And why is that? He doesn't know me."

"He's seen you in here and he asked Mike about you."

"I don't get this at all. How does any of this affect you? What's the favor?"

"Well," Leah began, "this guy, Brian, he has a nineteen fifty-seven Ford in mint condition. You know Mike, he wants that car so bad he can taste it. He told me that if he can get this car at a good price, we'll go shopping for my diamond. Brian will give Mike a bargain if he can see you."

Joy looked at Leah. "You aren't serious! Maybe you need to have a talk with Mike. I mean, come on Leah, the guy either wants to marry you or he doesn't. You've been together for what now, five years?"

Leah looked sheepishly at her friend.

"I don't believe this. You're pimping me out for a retro car."

Leah took a sip of her beer.

"Say something," Joy demanded.

"I'm sorry," Leah said.

"You should be."

The two girls sat there, one slightly angry, the other slightly scared. They looked around the room.

"Are you mad at me?" Leah finally asked.

Joy looked directly into Leah's eyes. "Oh, should I be?"

Leah looked as if she might cry. "I'd probably be mad at you," she said.

They spent the next few minutes in silence.

"Was there a time when I was supposed to meet this character? A place? What?"

"You'll do it?" Leah asked with surprise in her voice and eyes.

"I don't know. Answer my questions."

Leah squirmed in her seat. "Okay. He's twenty-eight and has a good job."

"You said that."

"Oh. Well, he's smart and he's decent. He'd like to meet you here where both of you are on familiar ground. Just have a beer or coffee at first, talk, get to know one another."

"When?"

"Tomorrow evening around seven, if that works for you."

Joy looked away and then back again at Leah. "Don't do this to me again."

"I won't."

Joy stood. "I'm tired. I'm going home."

"Okay," Leah said, "but there's just one thing. Look for a guy dressed in brown. All brown. He loves brown. Loves your brown hair, loved that brown outfit you wore, the one with the orange flecks in the skirt, loves brown."

"Oh, good," Joy said, and then she shoved her chair in and walked out of the bar and the three blocks to her apartment. She took a shower and changed into pale pink flannel pajamas and white socks. She glanced down at herself and thought she looked like a blushing rabbit. She went back to the card table and folding chair, turned on her laptop to check her emails, then resumed work on her clay horse. At midnight, she rubbed her eyes, threw a damp cloth over the completed creature, and went to bed.

The next day was a library workday, typical, coping with a few cranky patrons and decisions concerning budget woes and overdue books. Joy was not in the mood at all for the evening that Leah had planned for her.

At six-thirty she changed from her work clothes to jeans and a cranberry shirt. She would wear anything but brown. She decided against earrings; she had no interest in even attempting to interest this guy. Brian. Brown loving Brian. What a nut.

When she walked into The Pitfall, said hi to the bartender and then looked around, there he was, decked out in brown. A tan t-shirt showing its middle from a parted, brown zippered jacket. At least it isn't leather, she thought. She watched him for a few minutes as he sipped a dark ale and read a folded over newspaper. He didn't look up. She didn't exist in his present world, which made her wonder just what this guy was made of.

She took a deep breath and walked over to his table where she plopped her large purse and pulled out a chair to sit down. He looked across at her. She looked at him. "Well?"

His eyes were fastened on hers but he was silent.

Joy folded her arms across her chest. "Okay, I'll start. I want you to know that I don't appreciate this. You giving Mike a deal on your car, getting me to meet with you, that's a little strange and underhanded, don't you think?"

He continued to look at her.

"Do you speak? Come on. You could at least offer me a cup of coffee. A beer."

He looked into her fiery eyes and then waved to the bartender. "Could we get a beer over here, please?"

"Why did you choose a beer? I might have preferred a coffee."

"You need a beer."

Joy huffed and then the beer was placed before her. She stared at it and then drank half of it in a few swift gulps. She looked at him as she set the tall glass down on a coaster.

"So," she said, "I heard you like brown."

He looked at his jacket and down at his shoes. "I guess I do," he said.

"You know," she began, "it's pretty obvious that you have some peculiar tendencies. Have you ever contemplated therapy?"

He smiled. "Maybe I like having peculiar tendencies."

He's impossible, she thought and silently cursed Mike and Leah for asking this of her. And then she silently cursed herself for agreeing to it.

Joy watched him looking up at the soccer game playing on the huge TV. That inattention was insulting, but she had to admit, this guy, Brian, was one very good-looking man, brown hair and all. While she was studying his angular face, he suddenly turned back to look at her.

"So, what's your name?" he asked.

Joy half gurgled a response. "You don't know my name?"

He looked at her, not a glimpse of any emotion revealing his thoughts. "Unfortunately, I'm not psychic. But I could try to guess if you want."

Joy frowned. How, she wondered, could someone who looked so put together be so dense? "I don't like my name," she said, "but it's Joy."

34

He placed his newspaper down on the table. "What's wrong with Joy? It sounds perfectly fine to me."

"I don't like being an emotion, a feeling," she said.

"Another beer?" he asked.

"No, no thanks. But you were right, I needed the beer instead of more caffeine. It hit the spot."

He smiled and went back to watching the soccer game.

She watched him thinking how ridiculous this was. Why was he wasting his and her time like this?

When he glanced back at her, she was staring at him.

He smiled. "Are you okay? Can I get you something else? Would you like a sandwich or something?"

"No," she said as she sat up straight, her back to the wooden chair. "But I have to wonder, Brian, why you wanted to meet me when all you do is watch TV."

"Excuse me?"

"Well, come on. What's all this about?"

He looked at her then leaned forward. "My name isn't Brian."

Joy's body went rigid with an adrenalin rush. "What do you mean?"

"I mean that my name isn't Brian."

"Well then, who are you? Why did you carry on with me like this? You're wearing brown. You're not Brian?"

He smiled and shook his head no.

"Oh my...." Joy looked around at the other people in the bar. Where was Brian? The room was dimly lit, she saw no one in brown, no one alone. "This is ridiculous," she said. "Who are you?"

He tilted his body to one side and reached for his wallet. "Let me see," he said. "Well, my license says I'm James Cullen. Jim."

"Jim," she said, "just Jim?"

He smiled as she looked at his license and then he put it away. "Yup, just Jim."

"So, you're not an accountant for the state?"

"No."

"Where's Brian?"

He hesitated. "Is this like where's Waldo?"

Joy grimaced. "Do you know Brian?"

"Afraid not."

At that point, she looked around the room again, catching only a

35

glance at a man in brown hastily leaving the bar.

Joy put her hands over her face and moaned. "This is awful."

Jim chuckled.

"It's not funny," she said, and then found herself sitting there for the next hour explaining the entire situation and about half of her life. There was the divorce of her parents when Joy was eleven – the forced sale of the home she'd grown up in. There had been apartments and people she resented as part of her parents' new lives, and a couple of more than disappointing romances of her own. Joy was left mourning the trust she'd once known.

Jim studied her now somber face. "I think you need a get-a-way," he said, "a few days on Martha's Vineyard."

Joy listened. "Why Martha's Vineyard? I haven't been out there in years."

"Well then, it's time. I'll show you around. I live there, in Oak Bluffs, with a view of the harbor where the ferry comes in."

"You live there?"

"Sure. Why not?"

"I don't know. It just seems like a place to go for a few days."

"That's the invitation," he said with a smile.

"But you live there?"

Jim nodded. "Yes, I do."

"What do you do there?"

"Other than enjoy every moment of it, I'm a photographer. I do weddings, calendars, postcards, newspaper shots for a national press. I capture life."

Joy was silent. She captured life too, she realized, in her clay sculptures.

"So," he said as he looked into her eyes, "will you come out to my island?"

Joy looked at him and smiled as she heard herself reply, "Maybe… Yes."

"And you'll stay," he said with a completely serious voice and expression.

Joy looked down at her folded hands, then up into his very appealing face. "We'll see," she said.

# DELICIOUS

When the familiar sound of the brass mail slot squeaking open and clinking closed hit my flu-infected ears, I scuffed my way down the hallway with my uncombed hair, striped flannel pajamas, and monkey-face slippers to retrieve the usual assortment of bills and nuisance ads.

Today was different. Back in my apartment and there in my hands, I held a small packet, not sealed, wrapped in a plain, cream-colored envelope. It was addressed to *her*, Georgianna Moss, my snooty, highbrow neighbor in apartment Four A.

I turned the packet this way and that, snapshots falling like snowflakes all over my shiny oak floor. Ha! I picked up the first few and there she was, half dressed in a floozy shirt, the neckline down to her bony knees! Then another, the shirt off! I stooped and picked up the remaining photos and scuffed to the kitchen where I made tea while enjoying snorkeling laughter at revealing poses. Whew! "Who took these?" I questioned my cat, who was also smiling.

After tea, I walked the sizzling images to her door and dropped them through her monogrammed brass mail slot. Early that evening, I heard the unmistakable arrival of her Mercedes and waited to hear the key turn in the lock. I opened my door just a crack or two so that she could see me, then smiled a long one toward her haughty, unfriendly face.

And she wondered why.

# INSIDE OUT

## Outside

The near hurricane winds argued with the huge weeping willow in the front yard, with the twin sugar maples, the resistant and tall oaks, the supple pines, and tested the bravery of the one ancient chestnut.

Puddles from saturating rain gathered at the feet of all that stood still — the granite bench, the cast iron birdbath — and metal chairs toppled and slid gratingly across the patio flagstones, wet and glistening with strands of light from the log cabin's windows.

Twigs and freed leaves flew helplessly through the night sky, pinging at the roof, the doors, the windows. *Let me in, let me in.*

It was a fearsome night. No one in their right mind would want to be outside.

## Inside

The lights flickered and only the glow from the hearth lent a consistency to the room. Mia lit a candle just in case, then carried it with her to the kitchen where the flashlight waited in a drawer. She walked back to the hearth, placed another log on the fire, and noted that there were only two logs left inside. The woodpile in the shed would be dry when she needed more fuel, although she did not look forward to going out in the storm.

It was both comforting and sad to be in that old cabin by the lake, so many memories of summers there, and even some Thanksgivings. She recalled the sweet aroma of her mother's caramelized onions and hot dogs served with a zesty potato salad on a bed of homegrown lettuce. Mia smiled recalling her dad's old straw hat on the top of a small gold lampshade, creating a featureless face when the light was turned on, which earned a scowl from his wife. They bickered, they teased, and sometimes they were genuinely angry with one another, but they loved each other and Mia.

She walked to the left side of the hearth near a large window and sat down in her father's barrel-back chair. A flash of lightening projected itself into the room, the lights flickered again, and Mia drew her legs up and under her body, curling herself into the protective curved back and arms of the old recliner. The mechanism to lift the footrest no longer worked, but it was too comfortable for her father to have cast it out for a new one. She wanted them back. Ridiculously stubborn, she looked toward the fury-filled sky and told God that if he was really there, she wanted them back, *now.*

## Outside

From the cluster of swaying pines and resilient rhododendrons, the cabin was the essence of refuge. Golden beams reached out beyond the windows and spilled carelessly and invitingly onto evergreens and more rhododendrons, all rustling against the taunting wind. The windows were muted with streams of rain and leaves plastered against the glass. Inside, it would be warm and dry, *inside.*

## Inside

Mia braced herself against the sounds of the storm, the crackling of light and the shrieking wind. Her eyes sought the comfort of the hearth and grew heavy with the desire to sleep. She closed her eyes, her lips parted slightly as she tucked herself deeper into the chair's curve and slept. When she opened her eyes, it was because of a loud crash. Startled, she didn't move for a few moments, and then she slowly eased her legs to the floor and stood. With the flashlight in her hands, she went from room to room, looking for what could have made that sound. She found nothing. Feeling a little edgy, Mia walked back to the living room's hearth and sat down again, this time on the sofa, facing the window. The fire was glowing but fading. Mia stood and walked to the two remaining logs and placed them on the fire. She tucked a few pieces of kindling into the embers, then waited as the flames leaped and grew. She moved back to the sofa and wondered why she'd come up here alone.

## Outside

The rain was harsh, almost stinging to whatever it touched. The wind was unreasonably determined to have no direction, to toss and hurl, to tug and torture each victim in its way. Eyes blinked against the twirling pine needles and bits of twigs and grit. The lights from that cabin were intriguing.

## Inside

Just as the lights went out, Mia felt her heart twist as she saw what looked to be a face at the window. She froze, her eyes riveted to the blotch of yellow against the glass. She had not planned on any of this, not the storm, not being here alone, not the fear.

The lights came back within moments, then were lost again, but not before she could see that the yellow face at the window was really a clump of leaves clinging to the glass in desperation, fluttering like a giant moth pleading for help.

Now there was only the light from the small candle and the hearth. The whole place looked different; she'd never been there in a storm before, and especially not at night and not alone. She thought about making a cup of tea but decided not to move. Maybe the lights would come back. Mia didn't like the shadows in the darkened room; they seemed to take the life from it, just as the accident had taken life from her parents.

She was tired; it was after midnight now as she rested her head against the soft cushions. Then she looked to her right where the needlepoint pillow her mother had made as a gift to her father sat propped in the sofa's corner. It was a black background piped in moss green, a cluster of pine cones and acorns formed the intricate design. She touched it with her right hand, then lowered herself down on the sofa, drawing her legs up and allowing her head to rest on the pillow, the way as a child, she had rested her head in her mother's lap before sleep.

Mia woke up one hour later believing she'd heard a knock at the door. But who could possibly be out on a night such as this? She listened, her head raised now from the pillow, and then she sat up straight. She was cold, the late September air had prepared itself for the coming season and the dampness from the storm was penetrating. The fire was nearly gone, only little pops of sound came from the simmering logs, now aging into cinders. She stood, the lights were still out and the candle was low. She lit another candle and placed it on the mantle, then reached her arms into a jacket that had once belonged to her father. With the flashlight in her hand, she walked toward the door, then again, heard the sound of a knock. Mia felt the adrenalin rush through her chest and she took a step back into the room and listened. Then again, a knock, but this time, softer. She went to the window and switched the flashlight on, shining it toward the path that led to the front door. At first she was stunned by seeing something different, but then she realized that a large branch had been urged to the ground and was resting and bumping against the cabin and the door. With a sense of relief, she unlocked the door and braced herself for the strong winds and rain.

## Outside

She wanted to run the thirty or forty feet to the shed, but branches and other debris were scattered in such a way that she needed to watch her every step. When she reached the shed, she heard hinges squeak and with the flashlight shining on the usually stubborn old door, she saw that it was open and yielding to the storm. Mia had been teased over the years about the shed, always fearful that spiders or some other crawly thing might be waiting for her inside. She thought of that now, but she needed the wood for the fire. She stepped inside, put the flashlight down to rest as she began to gather as many logs as she could hold in her arms, and then the flashlight went dark. Motionless, she stood and listened, then backed out of the shed and made her way as best she could back toward the cabin. Within ten feet of the door, Mia saw that it was open. Had she not closed it properly? *Had someone gone inside?*

The wind and rain tossed her shoulder length hair and blew strands of it across her face and eyes. She dropped the logs to the ground, brushed her hair away from her face, and slowly stepped inside the cabin. She walked to her purse and car keys, blew out the candle on the mantle, and, terrified, walked to her car. Seeing the light go on inside when she opened the door was a relief and she glanced in the back seat and on the floor, then she sat behind the wheel and locked herself in. She pictured herself not being able to start the car, but it started fine, and the headlights provided an added comfort. Avoiding fallen branches as she drove, Mia felt sad that this wonderful cabin had at least temporarily lost its appeal.

## Inside

It was quiet in the cabin. The embers from the fire were smoking and some were still red. The front door was closed over, but not tight. Crackers and apples and a still wrapped meatball sub sat on the little round table in the kitchen next to a bottle of soda. He looked at the available food then tore open the white paper from the sub and ate most of it. He drank water from a half-filled glass in the sink. He looked around as best he could in the dark of that place, then made his way to the barrel back chair where he curled his ringed tail over his eyes and went to sleep.

(Published by Level Best Books, *Thin Ice*, 2010)

# SHOOT FOR THE MOON

James was away on business again. His absence didn't seem significant anymore. They had each sensed a restless loss in their relationship and had actually talked about downsizing their home after the kids finished college. Would they downsize their marriage as well?

Lauren and Michael were staying at their schools for the weekend. This seemed to be the usual lately, just *her* and the dog. This was not what she had ever hoped for. This was not even remotely a part of her dream. This was real and this was wrong, at least for her.

The aloneness, even when the family was there, was too much. They each lived in their own realm, as if they were closed in separate rooms with four walls and no doors to one another. Her room was getting very small and short of air. She felt the need to escape, to breathe.

She stood at the window, looking out beyond the raindrops on the glass. There, through muted panes, she could only see what she felt inside. Did anyone care? Would she ever be recognized beyond her family obligations and civic duties? Sometimes she invited in the thoughts of how it might be if someone were to take care of her. If someone wanted to, even a little bit.

With tears filling her eyes, she turned and walked to the stove where she poured hot water into a cup. She watched as the tea bag bobbed to the top then placed the kettle back on the stove. The warm cup felt soothing in her hands as she walked back to her place at the rain-spattered window. Steam from her tea added to the blur on the glass and her lips formed a slight, sad smile. That was sometimes the way life was; when things seemed bad enough, something else came along and made it worse.

Feeling suddenly chilled, she moved to the round table near the window, wrapped a sweater around her shoulders, then pulled out a chair and sat down with her tea.

A slight scratching at the kitchen door reminded her that Casey was outside in the rain. She stood, then walked to and opened the door to his

43

soft whimper and soaking wet body. He shook as he entered the kitchen. With a large towel, she dried his fur. "It's you and me, kiddo," she said to the wide-eyed dog. "No one else is home. Come on, I've got your dinner over here. Come and eat like a good boy." How many times had she used that same line with Michael who was now six feet plus and ate when and where he liked? Her creativity as a plotter and planner was now invalid. What was she doing? What was this life of hers all about anyway?

Leaning with her back against the sink, she watched as the dog, the puppy Michael begged for and vowed he would take care of *forever,* finished his food then sank comfortably on his rug bed in the corner.

"You're a good boy, Casey," she said as she knelt to gently stroke his moist head before going to her place again at the window.

"What am I doing with myself today?" she asked herself aloud, then she half laughed. "Today? I'm wondering about today, Casey? This cold and rainy Sunday? What about the *rest* of my life? Now *that's* a scary question!"

She moved away from the window and her cooling tea. "This is just dandy," she said to the sleepy-eyed dog. "My kids are more interested in staying at college than being at home, and my husband is off in the sunny west on business, and golf of course. Now let me tell you, Casey old boy, I'd be out there selling real estate today if it weren't for this cold October rain. Not even one call from a prospective buyer or seller. I mean, nobody wants to go out in the rain."

At the mention of *out*, Casey stood and wagged his tail approvingly.

"You've got to be kidding me," she said to the part sheepdog and part black-and-white something else. Casey sat but his eyes said that he wasn't kidding at all. He was ready to go. She laughed and said, "You know something, Casey, I think you're right. We could drive to the beach. I'll buy you a hot dog. What do you say?"

The dog woofed softly and wagged his tail in approval. With her pale blue raincoat securely buttoned, purse and keys in her hand, she opened the door for Casey and herself. As she locked the door, she had the distinct feeling that she was trying to lock away her emotions, at least for this trip to the beach. Worrisome thoughts and unanswerable questions could wait.

During their brief ride to the sandy shores, Casey sat in the front passenger seat, eager to be where he could run. "Okay, take it easy,

fella," she said as she parked the car facing toward the blue-green sea. "We're here, but don't you run off now. You stay near me or I'll have to put you on your leash. Got that?"

Casey suddenly stopped wiggling and was almost as still as a statue. She laughed and opened the car door. "Okay, go ahead, but keep your nose clean," she called out to the panda-like figure who had bounded out of the car and onto the wet sand.

As she stood outside her car, she realized that the rain had all but stopped. There was a soft mist and a breeze which reminded her to fasten the button at the top of her coat. As she closed her car door, her eyes followed Casey's form in the distance. He appeared to be running toward a smaller dog and a man, no doubt the small dog's owner. "Casey!" she called into the wind, then she walked out onto the sand, which molded her footprints near to Casey's. She walked steadily, not fearful of the two dogs meeting for she knew that although Casey was large, he was gentle. But after all, he *was* her responsibility. Why do I assume the responsibility for *everything*, even my dog's behavior? she wondered, amused with her own thoughts. She knew that deep inside she had always accepted that it was her business to see to it that Michael said 'thank you,' that Lauren said 'excuse me,' and that James wore the right shirt with the right tie. Now the kids were on their own and who knew if they acted like a gentleman and a lady when they were away from her? Did James wear the light green shirt with the dark green tie as she'd packed them? Did it really matter? It was now out of her hands. Her control was gone and here she was, on a wet beach with a wet dog and a stranger approaching her.

"Good afternoon," he greeted her from within a parka.

"Hello," she answered remembering her advice 'don't talk to strangers' she'd always used with Lauren.

"Our four-footed friends seem to like one another," he remarked as he reversed his direction and began to walk by her side. When she did not reply he continued, "Are you new around here?"

"I don't live at the beach," she said.

"You mean you actually drove here on this rainy day? I thought *I* was the only crazy person around here, but I guess I'm not."

She stopped and looked at the man's face, finding tanned skin and startlingly blue eyes. "Thanks so much," she said with a smile. "I *needed* someone to confirm my insanity."

45

He laughed then introduced himself. "I'm Dan Murphy. See that blue and white house over there?" He pointed to a tall, narrow house wedged in between two others that were red. "That's mine, at least for a while."

"It must be nice to live by the sea," she said.

"It's wonderful."

She walked, keeping her eyes on Casey and his newfound playmate.

"Do you have a name?" Dan asked.

"Doesn't everyone?" she replied with humor in her voice.

"Well, to tell you the truth, I thought *you* might be the exception," he said with a glance toward his companion's pretty face.

She smiled then brushed her blonde hair out of her eyes. "Maggie," she said.

"Maggie. Maggie. I *like* that. Where are you from, Maggie?"

"About three miles from here."

They were quiet for a few moments as they walked along on the firm yet giving sand. "And do you belong to someone other than Casey?"

Maggie hesitated then answered, "Not today. Today it's Casey and me."

"Okay, that's a fair answer I guess."

"You kind of indicated that you're here for *a while,*" Maggie said. "Are you a tourist enjoying the beach out of season?"

"Not really. I used to live here when I was a child. We moved when I was about seven, but I never forgot the place. When I needed a bit of peace and quiet, this was a natural choice. And in case you're wondering if I'm a lazy old beachcomber, I *am*, part time. I'm writing a book."

"What do you write?" Maggie asked.

"At present, a novel set during the Civil War period; that time has always interested and troubled me, one nation torn in two, hard times for all concerned."

"Sounds interesting. Is this a first novel? Have you written other things?"

"Yes, but nothing you'd recognize, I'm sure. I was teaching college and editing textbooks until three years ago. At that point I began to do some serious writing. I sold a few short articles on the Civil War and decided to shoot for the moon. So, here I am, with my facts and my

46

fiction on a beautiful stretch of New England beach."

Maggie stopped and looked at Dan's very pleasant face. "Does it make you nervous? I mean, writing. It seems like such an uncertainty. It must take some hefty fortitude to give up a secure job such as teaching."

Dan smiled. "You *bet* it makes me nervous. But, I've submitted my first few chapters to the house I've been editing for and they've given me some decent feedback. In my mind, that's a huge advantage."

"It sounds good," Maggie replied.

"So, what does Maggie-no-last-name do?"

"I sell real estate."

"Really? You don't seem the type."

"What type sells real estate?"

"Oh, people who are, um, *friendlier,*" he teased.

Maggie smiled but said nothing.

"How long have you been in real estate?"

"About ten years; it's been a good help with my kids' college tuition."

"So, Maggie *does* have a family other than Casey."

"I've a son twenty-two, a daughter twenty, and a husband who is a reluctant forty-six."

"I see. How about a nice, hot cup of coffee?" he asked as they approached a small take-out café. "I promised Barker a hot dog,"

Maggie laughed. "I promised Casey a hot dog too."

Sitting on a damp bench drinking their coffee Dan asked, "So, your life's not very fulfilling?"

"Did I say that?"

"Sort of. Do you like selling real estate?"

Maggie shook her head from side to side and stared out to a gray-green sea.

"Then why do you do it?"

Maggie took a sip of her coffee. "I don't know. I could make my own hours. It's been convenient, and the money has been decent."

"What do you *like* to do?" Dan asked. "Are you creative?"

"Not really, but I do have a passion for my herb garden and cooking. There is something I've often thought about though. Now don't laugh. I wanted to be a lawyer."

Dan was silent for a moment, his face serious. "So, why don't

47

you?"

"At *my* age? I'm forty-three years old. Can you see me in college?"

"Yes, I can," Dan replied. "Listen, even if you don't go all the way and become a lawyer, an education in that field could be interesting, challenging. You could do research for a law firm. And who knows, maybe you *would* decide to go for the bar. I'll bet you'd be a public defender or something."

Maggie smiled. He was right. She stood and walked to the trashcan where she deposited her empty cup. "I should be going," she said.

Dan stood up. "You were a nice surprise on a rainy day."

Maggie pulled a stray strand of hair away from her face. "Thanks, you were, too. Come on, Casey, time to go home." She began to walk toward her car.

"Maggie," Dan called to her and she turned to face him. "When you and Casey get back this way, knock on my door. Barker and I are always up for a walk on the beach."

She thought for a moment. "Casey and Barker seemed to enjoy one another, so why not?" Maggie turned around and started to walk, feeling the wet sand giving in to the patterned soles of her shoes. Impulsively, she turned around and stopped. "Dan? Good luck with your writing."

Dan waved. "Maggie? Good luck with your law studies, and remember, it's the blue house."

Maggie smiled and turned to walk on, Casey prancing at her side.

# TANGERINE

The heavy aroma of roasted garlic, sweet red peppers, the mingling of wine and beer, swirled with out-of-sync loud voices. All emphasized her need to escape that place, if only for a breath of fresh air. Anxiously lacing her fingers together, she looked around at the varying hues of orange, red, and gold decor, a smoky mist drifting into the room from the famed open-hearth kitchen of their once favorite restaurant. He was late again. *How like him to avoid confrontation. How like him to put another's importance for punctuality in a lesser space.*

She stood and moved her chair toward the table, betting the raucous atmosphere in that room that he simply wouldn't show. Gathering her purse to her shoulder, she went out through French doors to a bricked patio and the chilled air of an autumn night.

A man stood in the corner near a perfectly shaped spruce, the red glow from his cigarette offering the look of a miniature lantern. He glanced her way and nodded then, seeming to note her intrusion, he dropped the smoke and ground it into the brick with his shiny boot before leaving.

She shivered with the uncertainty of her future. They'd been together for three years. Good thing there had been no marriage, maybe. Or maybe there would have been a stronger commitment to that written document so easily dismissed when happily choosing a russet colored sofa, apricot draperies, and accessories in brilliant shades of red and orange.

He wasn't coming, she was sure.

She glanced at the flattened white remains of the man's cigarette then walked to the patio's edge where thick walls of waist high boxwood and holly grew, concealing a slight slope to the city sidewalk below and the lights. They seemed alive, those lights down there, among people holding hands who wanted to be together.

She turned around and glanced toward the French doors and her table, where she'd purposely left her tangerine silk scarf, a long-ago gift from him. No one else would take her place with that vivid marker and a half-filled glass of chardonnay. He'd see that scarf and know where to find her, if he came at all.

She turned again, noticing the people below on the sidewalk, bodies close enough to feel the heat from one another. Her chest, her legs, her shoulders ached for that agreed familiarity.

She blinked back a few tears. She could turn and walk through those doors one last time. She could retrieve the scarf then walk to her car and drive home. Home. Or she could push her way through the thick foliage and try not to stumble toward the sidewalk below.

With a deep breath, she stepped toward the boxwood. She did not turn around to see his lanky form standing at the table, the tangerine scarf draped in his hands.

# THE STORAGE UNIT

Daria danced around her best friend's kitchen, her arms high in the air like a ballerina's. "Come on, Caroline, can't you see what fun this could be? All that stuff in those units, we could find anything, even Jimmy Hoffa!"

Caroline laughed and shook her head. "You're crazy; look at this place. Does it look like I need a storage unit full of junk? Especially Jimmy Hoffa, now what would I do with him, have him stuffed as a conversation piece?"

"Oh, cut it out! Let's just do it. I've heard about these storage sales from my aunt and uncle for years. They have a ball at them; they've gotten some really great bargains. Their cherry dining room set for instance, and that Haviland china, good deals."

"I'll tell you what. I'll go with you," Caroline said, "but I probably won't buy a unit myself. I'll just keep you company."

Daria smiled. "Okay, I'll settle for that."

Two days later, on a misty gray day, the girls set off on their adventure. Daria was animated with expectation while Caroline smiled through the drive to the city. They stood in line and were given a number. It was amazing to Caroline how many people showed up to purchase a "grab bag." One by one, the units were claimed and sold, until there were only three units remaining and no buyers clamoring for them.

"This is a sign, Cary. You should buy one of the units, then we can go and check them out, see what we have."

Caroline grimaced then made an offer for the contents of number one hundred-seventy-one. It was hers.

Daria's unit was the first to be investigated. It revealed an interesting array of furniture. "Look at this wicker set," she said. "This will be perfect in my new apartment. A few of these lamps are a little more retro than my taste, but, still, they're interesting."

When the girls moved to Caroline's unit, they found it filled with dollhouses of every style and color imaginable.

51

"Wow!" Daria said. "Look at all of these; they look hand crafted."

Using only the light from the garage-size door, Caroline's eyes scanned the room. She walked further into the unit and touched a house here and there, admiring the smoothness of the wood and the intricate workmanship, but wondering what she was to do with so many dollhouses. They were appealing to her, like little works of art.

"You could probably sell these for a fortune to some toy store," Daria said. "In fact, my niece's birthday is next month; I'd love to get one for her."

"Sure," Caroline said, "pick out the one you want and it's yours. Honestly, I might give one as a gift too, but I think I'll see if a charity wants the rest of them for auctions or raffles. They really are beautiful."

"Great idea. We'll borrow Danny and his truck later and we'll move all this stuff. We've got until tomorrow at five to get everything out of here."

Caroline agreed. She walked among the dollhouses and stopped at one that resembled a little gingerbread cottage, painted a blush pink with white shutters and trim. The door was a cranberry color, and over it was carved a date, November 1st, 1953.

"This one is dated," she said to Daria, and then they noticed that they were *all* dated.

"This one is dated November 1st, 1959," Daria said. "It looks like they're all dated November first, with different years."

Caroline moved around the room, her eyes still drawn to the pink cottage. She noticed a stack of papers, many browned with age, tied with a black satin ribbon. She picked them up and, along with what looked like letters, was a yellowed newspaper clipping. She took it closer to the doorway to read it as Daria followed.

"Oh, my God," Caroline said softly. "This is the obituary for a little girl named Emma. She was days away from being four when she died in a car accident on October 28th in 1953. That's the date, nineteen fifty-three, on that little pink cottage over there." Then one after the other, they checked the dates on each letter, beginning with 1953 and ending 2005.

Daria was quiet for once, seeming forlorn over the loss of the child.

Caroline turned her attention to the letters and looked through them to see that each one was decorated with tiny hearts and stars. They began the same, "To my Darling little Emma, on your birthday," and each one was signed, "With all my love forever and ever, Papa."

The two friends sat down on the cement floor of the unit, each one taking several pages, all chronologically arranged. When they were through reading each of the fifty-two letters, they both had tears in their eyes.

"This is the saddest thing I've ever known," Daria said. "This father made his little girl a new doll house every year for her birthday, even after she'd died, as if he was in complete denial or something. I wonder if he passed away after making the one for 2005."

Caroline nodded and brushed away the tears as she again scanned the room and its emotional contents.

"I'll keep the pink one," she said. "I loved it when I saw it, and it's the one he made for her first, for her fourth birthday. You take whatever others you want for your nieces or whoever, and I'll call around to some of the charities. Maybe even Children's Hospital."

"I guess I'll take the red one for my niece," Daria said as she lifted it and walked to Caroline's trunk.

Caroline moved the pink cottage to her car and then selected a second house, a pale yellow one, as a gift. She placed it next to the pink house and smiled at the little neighborhood she'd created in her backseat.

After dropping Daria and her dollhouse off, Caroline ran a few errands before going home. She carried in her few groceries and her suit from the dry cleaners before she returned to the car. The pink dollhouse was perched on the backseat, looking as if it was waiting for her. Caroline reached in carefully, not wanting to scrape it or crack its delicate trim. She smiled, thinking how beautiful it was, but then she remembered Emma and was sad for the child and the grief of the father. Until he grew too old to remember, or had died himself, he'd kept this child as the focus of his love.

She took the pink cottage in and placed it on a cabinet across from her sofa. Then she returned to her car for the yellow house and left it in the study until she could give it to her cousin's daughter. After putting her groceries away, Caroline sat on the sofa and closed her eyes. It was late afternoon, close to six when she fell asleep. When she awoke, the room was dark, except for the dollhouse, every room was alight. Caroline squinted disbelievingly, then walked to the house and looked inside. A little chandelier over the dining room table was illuminated; a light over the kitchen sink was on; two little lamps in the master bedroom were brightly lit on each side of the bed, and a lamp near the fireplace in the living room was cheerful with light through a garnet-colored shade. Caroline took a step back then looked for a sign of electricity. She could see no wires, and certainly, she had not plugged it in. Puzzled, she walked back to the sofa and sat down looking at the dollhouse.

The phone rang. Daria was reminding her that she and her fiancé and Caroline and her boyfriend were meeting at eight for a night on the town. Caroline hurried to get dressed then left for an evening of fun and an overnight at Daria's. When she returned home in the morning, the lights in the pink house were out. She smiled. Must have been dreaming, she thought.

By five that afternoon, the contents of the two units had been carefully moved. The remaining dollhouses were taken to a grateful hospital where most would be raffled off, and then each of the four friends went to their own homes.

Dark outside, only Caroline's porch light beckoned her. Stepping into her living room, her hand on the light switch, she hesitated as she saw that the dollhouse was lit.

Caroline called Daria and asked, "I'm just curious, the doll house you have, are the lights on?"

Daria laughed. "Oh, sure, and there's supper in the tiny oven too."

Caroline was silent for a few moments. "You have no lights at all?"

Daria was quiet for a moment. "Well, there are little lamps and fixtures, but they aren't lit up or anything. Why?"

Caroline looked at her illuminated dollhouse. With the portable phone in her hand she walked to the study to look at the yellow house she would give as a gift. There was nothing but darkness there.

She said goodbye to Daria then sat down across from the pink cottage. In a quiet whisper she said, "*Happy Birthday, Emma.*"

# ERICA

She walked, her large sunglasses hiding her eyes and thoughts. She was alive, but it seemed that nothing and no one else was. Even the sun, as if not yet born, was concealed behind a huge grey-blue cloud. Her stride was swift, steady, unyielding.

"Excuse me, Miss, may I take your luggage?" the porter questioned.

"What? I'm sorry, did you say something to me?" she asked.

"Your luggage, Miss. May I help you with it?"

She looked down at the large leather case at her side. "Yes, please. It's BOAC, flight four-twenty."

"Yes, Miss. This way, please."

Quietly she followed the porter to the check-in desk.

"May I help you?" asked a young woman who systematically tore tickets apart and separated them into neat compartments.

"Yes, I have a reservation on flight four-twenty to Paris."

The young woman consulted her wristwatch and then the large clock behind her. "Flight four-twenty doesn't leave for another three hours, but I'll take your luggage for you. What is your name please?"

"Erica Hand."

The young woman efficiently marked and separated a ticket, then curtly placed it on the counter in front of Erica. "Gate nineteen in about one and a half hours. Have a pleasant flight," suggested the British accent.

Erica placed the ticket in her shoulder purse and walked toward gate nineteen.

Alone in the lounge area, she sat down and removed her sunglasses. The runway was busy with baggage wagons and fuel trucks crisscrossing one another in the morning fog. She rubbed her eyes, wishing that thoughts could be rubbed away and soothed in the same manner. As she discovered that people were now sitting nearby, Erica replaced the sunglasses and sat quietly.

"Good morning," the nun began with a cheerful smile.

"Good morning," Erica replied softly.

55

"You're American, aren't you?" the nun inquired.

"Yes, I am."

"Ah," the nun began. "I visited your country four years ago. Lovely place. Are you in England on holiday?"

Erica hesitated. "No, I've lived here for some time."

What was she doing here anyway, sitting in Heathrow Airport? Why was she running away again? Erica understood that whenever life became too complicated for her, the urge was there to flee. Looking up again, several other people had taken seats around them as they waited for their flights to be called. The nun had begun a conversation with someone else and Erica was glad not to have to converse with anyone. She hoped that her seat on the plane would not be next to a talker.

When the flight announcement was made, she walked, her back straight, to the aircraft where she found her window seat.

The engines began to hum, then to scream, and then the white lights on the moist runway blended together into a solid streak as the plane raced along the ground in preparation for flight.

Cotton-like clouds replaced the precise patchwork of the earth below and Erica thought how like herself it all was; closing out what she did not care for in life came easy to her. Clouds masked the height, giving the illusion of being only inches from solid footing. Erica rested her head back against the seat and closed her eyes.

Paris was alive with golden lights and early morning traffic as she made her way to a waiting taxi and on to the small apartment of a friend. It would be good to see Lauren again. She'd been an important part of Erica's life since childhood. The taxi came to an abrupt halt before a pink stone building and jolted her thoughts to the present, to the problems and pain she felt in her heart. Erica took her suitcase from the seat next to her and stepped out onto the sidewalk.

"Erica, you're welcome here anytime," Lauren assured her as she poured two cups of black coffee and placed them on the kitchen table before her friend.

"Thank you. I really didn't want to bother you, but I didn't know where else to go. I'll find a place later today. Any suggestions?"

"Sure, you'll stay right here."

Erica shook her head. "No, I couldn't do that."

"Yes, you can. Look, I'm leaving here tomorrow for a solid month. It's time for my annual 'See? I'm okay visit.' I dread going. Mom and

56

Dad usually expect something significant to have happened, and by their standards, nothing has."

"I know," Erica smiled. "I have the same problem."

"Are you still working at the embassy in London?"

Erica stood and walked to a window overlooking a narrow street. "Yes, I'm on leave. I just felt the need to get away for a while."

"Josh Kinney?" Lauren asked.

Erica removed her sunglasses then faced Lauren with swollen brown eyes. "Not Josh. Me." Erica answered flatly.

"God, Erica, your eyes look awful! What's going on?"

"I've cried myself silly for three days. Josh and I won't be seeing each other anymore."

"What happened? I thought you two were pretty serious."

"I thought so, too, but I was wrong."

"Well, why? What's happened?"

Erica smoothed back her short dark hair and sat down across the table from Lauren. "He's bringing his daughter over."

"His daughter? Didn't his wife have custody?"

"Yes, but she, Kathy, wanted to see Josh. She's going to attend school in London for at least this year."

"Does that really matter so much, Erica?"

"Yes, it does. Josh and I were really good for each other, Lauren, but I can't take a third entity. How do I compete with a ten-year old child?"

"Who decided there'd be a competition? Did Kathy give you that impression?"

"Kathy? I haven't even met Kathy. She arrives today."

"Oh, Erica! You're nuts!"

"Am I? Maybe I am, I just don't know anymore."

"Look," Lauren began, "Josh Kinney is one in a million. His little girl can't be all that bad! I think you've really jumped the gun this time."

"I don't know."

"Erica, sometimes things *do* work out! I don't want to sound cruel, but try to think back to other instances. Your parents wanted a career for you, so instead of failing them before their eyes, you took a Civil Service job away from home. When Phil Techner wanted you to marry him, rather than cope with his feelings, you traded your job in

Washington for the one in London. Now it's Josh. It's not real to do this, Erica."

Erica sat silently, her somber eyes transfixed on a moth on the outside of the windowpane.

"I'm sorry," Lauren said. "I've said too much. I'm no help."

"No, you're right about me. I was thinking about myself earlier today and I know I'm a quitter. I'm so intimidated by life, it's ridiculous."

"I'm intimidated sometimes, too, Erica. But that's the way it is, you still have to push on, to adjust."

\*\*\*

Seated in a small coffee shop in Heathrow Airport, Erica made mental notations to herself. A taxi back to her apartment, a call to Josh. In a mirror before her, Erica abstractedly watched people in the gift shop behind her. A small girl caught her eye. The child was, perhaps, Kathy's age. Erica watched as the slim girl reached up to a shelf slowly, gently, to stroke a large, white fluffy teddy bear with sparkling blue glass eyes. She seemed in awe of her surroundings.

When the child moved out of sight, Erica paid for her coffee and left the shop. The small girl sat alone near a window overlooking a runway. Her small hands were clasped at one moment tightly together, and the next moment, a ring was slid on and off her thin finger.

Erica watched from a distance. The child was obviously alone, and possibly Kathy. *Could* this small, nervous, insecure little girl be Kathy? She *was* due to arrive today.

Erica turned and walked down the highly polished hallway to the gift shop. It really didn't matter if that was Kathy or not. Any child would be naturally apprehensive after traveling alone for several hours. Kathy was accepting a new and strange environment to be with her father, a concession Erica might not have made at Kathy's age.

The taxi driver took Erica's luggage and placed it in the front seat, then opened the rear door for Erica. "Shall I take him up here with me, Miss?" He inquired politely.

"No, thank you," Erica smiled. "He's a friend for a friend. I think I'll just hold onto him." The fluffy, white, comical-faced bear sat perched on Erica's knees.

# SUNDAY BRUNCH

"I don't think this would be easy for you, Minna," he said. "This kid is different, kind of wild looking."

Minna squirmed in her chair and placed her tea cup down on the Formica-topped café table. "What do you mean by wild looking?" she asked.

Ben took a sip of lukewarm coffee, placed his cup down to mimic hers, then said, "Oh, you know. He wears a black leather jacket and jeans just about all the time. And tattoos, they're all over his arms and God knows where else."

Minna patted her lips with a paper napkin and looked into her friend's deep brown eyes. "Tattoos against the law?"

Ben half smiled and sighed. "Come on, Minna, you're the straightest arrow I've ever known. You like the clean-cut type."

"Like you."

Ben chuckled as he looked down at his own attire. "Well, yeah, chino pants and a starched shirt."

Minna looked at Ben with no reply.

"Hey," he said, "have you fallen out of love with me?"

Minna's lips gave way to a smile and then laughter.

Ben laughed too. "Well?" he said.

"Never," she answered. "But don't go telling your parents about us."

Ben laughed again.

"Look," she said, leaning slightly forward, "I appreciate your concerns for me, but I'm going to be seventy-two in a few months. Don't you think I can handle a few tattoos and a kid in leather?"

Ben sat back in his chair, arms folded across his chest, and gave her a quiet smile.

"Your parents are among my dearest friends, Benjamin. I adore and trust you, but I trust me too. I detest living in that big old house by myself, and I have no interest in downsizing. I want a boarder. If this kid is willing to do a few things around the house when needed, and he's agreed to no women in his room, I'd like to meet him. Make the arrangements for me. How bad can he be? He's at the university and one of your students. Come on, Ben."

Ben shook his head and then smiled. "Okay," he said. "I'll set up the introduction and you can decide. Right now, I'd better get home to my wife and kids before I'm suspected of keeping time with an attractive older woman."

They each stood and shoved their chairs to the table.

"Give them my love," Minna said.

One week later, Minna Oliver opened her Brazilian Mahogany front door to find herself staring at a tall, lanky young man in a black leather jacket, jeans, and worn looking sneakers. She glanced at his head where he wore a dark blue knitted cap which he pulled off, revealing thick, dark hair. She was speechless. He was incredibly attractive in an untraditional way. With finely chiseled features, it was hard to tell if he was Irish, Native American Indian, or something she hadn't thought of.

"Hi," he said. "I'm John."

Minna swallowed then composed herself before she reached out a hand to him. "And I'm Minna," she said. "Come in, John."

He stepped inside and looked around. It wasn't a mansion, but it was a bigger house than any he'd lived in before. His pale blue eyes scanned the wide, polished moldings and the staircase with a balcony above.

"This is nice," he said.

Minna liked his gentle demeanor. "Thank you. Hang your jacket over the banister there and have a look around. You like tea? I was just making some."

"Do you have coffee?" he asked.

"No," she said. "I'm sorry. Tea?"

"That's okay. Thanks anyway."

Minna hesitated, wondering if they were off to a rough start. "Well, you can still take a look around while I tend to my tea. If you want to see what would be your space, there are two rooms upstairs on the left, and the bathroom. I figured you could use one room for your bedroom and the other for a sitting room."

John nodded.

"I suppose that's not a term folks use these days," she said. "What I mean is, you could keep a TV and maybe a computer in one of the rooms."

"Sure, that's a good idea," he said with a smile.

Minna turned and walked down the hall to her kitchen.

John walked to the left into a formal looking living room, no TV. He then walked out of that room and to the right of the front door into a dining room rich with a gleaming dark table and chairs, a glass cabinet, and clipper ship works of art framed against a Wedgewood blue wall.

Minna returned, her hands folded, no tea.

"Have you been upstairs?"

"No. Would you mind?" he gestured toward the steps.

"Have a look," she said.

John nodded and climbed the stairs. When he came back down, Minna was sitting in her living room holding a mug of steaming tea.

"What did you think?" she asked.

John raised his eyebrows and smiled as he looked up at the ornate ceiling and then back to Minna's bright hazel eyes.

"It's nice," he said. "I think this would work great for me if …."

"Okay, then," Minna said. "When will you be moving in?"

"Tomorrow?" he asked.

Minna wasn't expecting things to move so fast, but then, why prolong the inevitability of change?

"Here," she said as she stood and took a key from a shelf, handing it to him. "If I'm not here, I do a little volunteer work, just let yourself in. You'll need a key anyway. There's just one thing I want to be certain that you understand; no women in your rooms. I asked Professor Lind to tell you that."

"Yes, Ma'am, he did, and that's fine."

"Okay then. I'll see you tomorrow, John."

He turned, slipped his tattooed arms into the sleeves of his leather jacket, and pulled the knitted cap over his hair. He walked toward the door and turned. "Would it be all right if I brought some coffee to make in your kitchen?"

Minna took note again of the angular face, the deep-set eyes. "Yes, of course. You may use the kitchen all you want. Do you perk your coffee? I have a coffee pot. My husband used to like a cup once in a while."

"That would be great," he said, "as long as you don't mind."

"I don't mind," she said, but as he turned to go and when he'd left, she thought of how coffee had a way of sending its aroma into other rooms and how it would remind her of Henry, of them, and she knew it would make her almost sick.

Two mornings later, with the wafting of rich coffee meeting her at the top of the stairs, Minna took a deep breath, closed her eyes, then opened them and took her first step down. Obviously, he'd risen early and found the coffee pot.

"Hi," he said with a smile as she entered the kitchen to see smoke from the toaster circling the old tin canister set. "I made coffee and I have whole grain toast. Would you like some?"

"No," she said. "Thank you, John. I'll make some tea. Did you sleep well?"

"Like a rock," he said.

"Good. Do you have classes today?"

It was Saturday, she didn't think he would, but he had his valise and papers on the table.

"No, no classes for me on weekends, but I'll be heading out to the library to use a computer."

"You don't have one?" Minna asked as she dropped a tea bag into a cup of steaming water.

"No," he said.

"I thought everyone did," she said, and then added, "I even have one. You're welcome to use it; it's in the study next to the living room. The door's not locked – I do a few emails once or twice a week, but that's about it. And I have a TV in there too. It's a small room, cozier than the parlor. I like a little TV once in a while – PBS has some good stuff."

John looked at her and smiled as he sat down with his buttered toast and coffee. "Thank you," he said. "I might take you up on those offers."

"Is that all you eat for breakfast?" she asked.

"Usually. It's pretty fast and easy," he said. "How about you? What do you eat for breakfast?"

Minna sat down across from him at the small round table. "I have tea, then after an hour or so, I have a little fruit and a cookie."

John laughed and nodded his approval.

"I hope you don't expect meals," she said. "I don't cook."

John swallowed a piece of toast and lifted his cup of coffee. "Oh, I don't expect meals, Ma'am, not at all. You don't cook?"

"No, I don't."

"What do you eat?"

Minna shrugged her shoulders. "I used to eat at the university cafeteria when I taught there, but since I retired, I've been picking up whatever I can pop in the microwave. I manage."

"I cook," John said. "I love to make breakfast food, but I like all cooking."

"That's good," she said.

John finished his toast and swallowed the remainder of his coffee.

"I used to make Sunday brunch when I lived in Oregon," he said.

"You're from Oregon?"

"Yes."

"That's a hike away from New England."

"Yes, it is."

"So, who'd you make brunch for, some lovely young lady?"

John shook his head from side to side. "No, for my family."

"Well, they must miss you," Minna said.

John wiped butter from his full lips. "No, not really. My mother died three years ago, and my father met someone a year after. I never thought he would, at least not so soon. Anyway, when she moved in, I moved out. I decided to come east, and here I am."

"So, you cooked for your mother?"

John nodded. "Yes. It was kind of a treat for her, and a tradition to do the Sunday brunch."

"That sounds very nice," Minna said, then she thought about Henry and their son, Gregory. They'd enjoyed sharing good meals together too.

"I have an idea," John said. "How about if I pick up a few things after the library and I can make us a nice little brunch tomorrow?"

"Oh," Minna said, "that's not necessary. I'm fine with my little routine, and you've got your studies. But thank you, John, it's a nice offer."

When Minna opened her eyes on Sunday morning, she could smell cinnamon. She lay in her bed, eyes to the ceiling, then tossed the covers aside, got up and dressed. After making her bed, she walked to the stairs and heard John's voice.

"Ma'am, would you step into my sitting room please?"

Minna touched the star-shaped brooch at her throat then turned and walked into a room that had been rearranged to accommodate a twin bed being used as a sofa, and a table and chairs before a window, set with coffee, a cup of tea, scrambled eggs, and cinnamon buns.

"What's all this?" she asked.

John smiled as he beckoned for her to sit at the table. "I thought it might be fun for us to have this time together on Sundays."

Minna wondered as she sat down if he was missing home. "Well, this is a lovely surprise," she said. "Thank you, John."

"You're welcome," he said. "Would that be okay with you, Sunday brunch? We could have it right here, just like this. It's kind of nice using this room to entertain."

Minna smiled. "I suppose I don't qualify as having a woman in your rooms."

John laughed. "I'm honored to have your company, Ma'am."

Minna huffed. "Goodness, John, stop calling me Ma'am. The name is Minna."

"Minna," he repeated. "So, Minna, would you allow me to prepare brunch for us on Sundays?"

Minna smiled. "I don't see why not." She took a mouthful of eggs and couldn't wait to sink her sweet tooth into a cinnamon bun. "Did you make those from scratch?" she asked.

"No, I made these from a package you pop open and bake, but if I pick up flour, sugar, things like that, I can do better than these."

Minna took a sip of hot tea and thought about how it had been five years since she last had baking ingredients in the house. "This is delicious," she said.

John offered his guest a cinnamon bun and she accepted.

"I have a question you're not allowed to ask *me*, John. How old are you?"

John smiled. "Twenty-three."

Minna nodded. "Did you go to school, college, in Oregon?"

"Yes, for two years. When my mother got sick, someone needed to take care of her, and there was no money anyway. After she died, I worked for a while and then I came here."

"I'm glad you did; it's nice having you here," Minna said, and she meant it.

The first full week of their living together went smoothly, but Minna was on the lookout for the possibility of a problem. There was

64

none.

When Sunday came around again, Minna opened her eyes to smell coffee. She wrinkled her nose then moved from her back to her side with agility, placing her bare feet on the plush rug next to her bed. She wasn't going anywhere; it was mid-November and cold. She pulled on a pair of powder blue slacks and a thick tan sweater, ran a brush through her curly blonde-gray hair, and stepped out into her hallway where she walked toward the stairs.

"Good morning, Minna," John said as he stood at his sitting room doorway.

Minna stopped and looked at her young boarder. "Good morning, John."

He gestured toward the table in his room set with dishes, food, and a teapot. "It's Sunday," he said as if to remind her. "I have brunch all ready for us."

Minna tugged at the cuffs of her sweater. "You're spoiling me, John. This smells wonderful."

Minna walked into the room and, as John pulled a chair out for her, she sat down.

"What smells so good?"

John lifted tin foil from a plate revealing eggs over easy on toast with melted cheddar. On another plate, he had clusters of grapes and two frosted cookies.

Minna smiled. "This is very artistically done, John, very appealing."

"Thank you," he said, his bared tattoos in plain view as he moved to pour tea into Minna's cup.

Her eyes went to his lean arms and she noticed that he was aware of that. Neither of them commented on the colorful artwork displayed on his firm, young skin. He smiled and offered fruit to go with her eggs.

"What are you studying, John?" she asked as she sliced her food into small pieces. "And how are your studies going?"

He placed a handful of grapes on his plate then looked up at his guest. "Everything's good. I'm actually doing a Liberal Arts program with a leaning toward business."

"Business?"

"Yes, does that surprise you?"

Minna sipped her tea then commented on the excellent food. "Not much surprises me," she said, "but I must admit, business wouldn't have been my first guess."

"What would have been?" he asked.

Minna took another bite of egg and toast, thought about it, then said, "Something creative I guess."

"Can't business be creative?"

Minna shrugged and took a sip of tea. "Sure, I suppose so. Do you have a plan?"

John placed his fork down on the plate. "I think I'd like to own and operate a restaurant."

Minna peered at John over the rim of her tea cup. "Now that doesn't surprise me a bit. Would you do the cooking?"

"Some of it; I'd probably sweep the floors at first too."

"Nothing wrong with that," Minna said.

"What about you?" he asked.

"What about me?" she said.

"This is a big house," he observed. "You mentioned a husband. What do you like to do?"

Minna dabbed at her lips with a napkin. "Henry passed away about five years ago."

John's eyes scanned Minna's pleasant face. "I'm sorry."

Minna shrugged. "Things happen," she said softly.

"Any children?" he asked.

Minna shifted in her chair. "We had Gregory, our son."

John heard her say the word *had* and he was quiet.

Minna stood, thanked John for the breakfast feast, then pushed her chair in, and walked toward the door.

John looked as though he'd like to ask more. He wondered but decided to save additional questions for another time.

On an early December Saturday afternoon, there was a knock at Minna Oliver's front door. She had been upstairs and was almost at the bottom of the staircase as John met her in the hallway coming from the kitchen.

She opened the door to see a smiling woman Minna recognized from the neighborhood.

"Mrs. Oliver," the attractive forty-something woman began, "I'm Kerry Albert; I live diagonally across the street."

"Oh, yes," Minna said. "Hello."

"Maybe you know about our street being chosen for the Christmas

66

Eve luminaries. We're hoping that each home will cooperate in decorating and wondered if you'd like any assistance or suggestions."

Minna stood perfectly still. "No," she said firmly. "I do not celebrate Christmas. I won't be decorating."

The look on Kerry Albert's face was one of shock and disappointment. "Could we persuade you to hang a simple wreath on the door, Mrs. Oliver?"

"No," Minna said politely. The two women were silent before Minna said, "Good day, Mrs. Albert," and closed the door.

She turned to see John standing just three feet behind her, looking thoughtful but saying nothing.

Minna met his eyes briefly then walked into her kitchen to make tea. The aroma of coffee met her and she found that she was getting used to it; in fact, she didn't mind it at all.

John walked into the kitchen and stayed out of her way as she moved about getting water in her cup. As she placed it in the microwave and stood watching the cup turn, he poured himself a cup of coffee.

Minna took her tea to the table and sat down. They said nothing to one another then John pulled out a chair and sat down across from her. He stole quick glances at Minna's face. She focused on her bobbing tea bag, then squeezed it against the cup and removed it to the saucer.

When they'd each consumed about half of their warm drinks, Minna asked what John was doing for the weekend.

"Not much," he said. "I have a paper to write and work tonight from six to closing. I'll try to be quiet when I come in; it'll be late, probably after midnight."

Minna nodded. "John, I'm up until one or two most nights reading. Don't worry about being quiet for me."

He watched as she finished her tea and took her cup and saucer to the sink where she washed it and left it to dry on the drain board.

"I'm going to run an errand," she said. "Is there anything I can pick up for you while I'm out? There's a great bakery down the street. What do you like? I'll buy you a cupcake or something – chocolate or vanilla?"

John smiled as he moved his cup, watching the swirling coffee, then he lifted his eyes to Minna's. "I don't eat too many sweets, but my weakness is cheesecake. Once in a while I like chocolate, really good chocolate."

Minna liked those things too, but she didn't reveal that information. She thought about Henry and Gregory; they'd both loved cheesecake with a spoonful of hot fudge sauce flowing over the top and down the sides.

"Well," she said, "I'll no doubt see you later then."

John nodded. "Is there something I can do to help out here? Vacuum? Anything?"

"It's good of you to offer, John, but a woman has been coming in once a week for years. You'll meet her one of these days, I'm sure. I don't mind dusting, but vacuuming isn't my thing. What I'd really like to depend on you for are those quirky little things, like stubborn hinges and door knobs that come loose. And, of course, it's just nice to have another person in the house at night."

"Okay," he said, and then Minna left.

When she had gone, John took his cup to the sink as she had, washed it, and left it to dry on the drain board. He looked out at drifting snowflakes then went up to his rooms.

The next morning, Minna twitched her nose at the aroma of John's coffee. She dressed, made her bed, tip-toed downstairs to the kitchen, then went back upstairs carrying a white pastry box.

John opened his sitting room door and smiled. "Welcome to Café John," he said as one arm beckoned toward the table set with an ample tray of scrambled eggs, sliced melon, golden brown toast, a pot of tea, and a mug of coffee.

Minna smiled. "I know I've claimed this before, but it's true, you're spoiling me, John. But," she said holding the box out to him, "I have something to contribute that I think you'll like."

John raised his dark eyebrows and opened the box to find a generous slice of cheesecake, chocolate drizzled over the top, adorned with a huge strawberry.

"Wow," he said, "this looks decadent."

Minna laughed. "Yes, I suppose it is."

"We'll share it," he said. "This is great."

"You're young and slim, and cholesterol probably hasn't caught up to you. I'll enjoy watching *you* eat it."

"If you please," he said as he pulled Minna's chair out for her, then tucked his guest into a comfortable position.

"This is lovely, John. You're a natural with food preparation."

John sat down and swallowed a mouthful of eggs, then reached for his coffee.

"May I ask you something?"

"Sure," Minna replied. "Go ahead."

John hesitated, looked out through the window next to their table at flakes of snow, then looked into Minna's eyes. "Why do you shun Christmas? Is it a religious difference?"

Minna patted her lips with a napkin and looked down at her plate before looking back at John's handsome face. "No, I'm not religious. I'm not anti-religion either," she said, not wanting to offend John in case he had a strong belief system. "I just don't do Christmas any longer."

John nodded, hesitated, then asked, "Could you tell me why? I mean, I don't want to pry, but, well, I just wondered."

Minna looked around the room. It was tidy, even with stacks of books here and there. "My son," she said, "he died in a car crash one week before Christmas the year he turned twenty. I haven't celebrated since then. That was twenty-five years ago."

John swallowed a bite of toast and said nothing. He thought that twenty-five years was a long time to suffer so deeply.

Minna took note of the look in John's eyes. "I suppose you like the holidays."

"Yeah, I do," he said carefully.

"Are you going home for Christmas?"

John shook his head. "This is home," he said with a crooked little smile.

Minna looked at him and nearly cried. "*This* is home? *My* House?"

John smiled, but his eyes reflected sadness. "Yeah, it feels like that to me. Home is a pretty meaningful word. I think this feels more like home than anything I ever knew before."

Again, Minna worked hard not to shed tears.

"Would you," John began, "be okay with me putting up a tree?"

"A Christmas tree?"

John smiled, "Yeah."

Minna took a sip of tea then stood slowly. "You may decorate your rooms any way you wish, John. Thank you for another delightful brunch. Everything was delicious."

69

John stood to walk with her to the doorway. With Minna gone, he closed the door and cleared the table. He looked out at the gray skies then sat down with a book and a pad of paper for notes.

Three days later, Minna was about to turn into her driveway when something caught her eyes. She slowed the car to a crawl and looked up to one of John's windows. There, for the neighborhood to see, Minna's eyes found the colorful lights of a Christmas tree behind the window of his sitting room. At first she felt a pang of anger, then she sighed as she recalled telling him that he could decorate his rooms as he wished. She hadn't thought that he'd place a tree at the window – she hadn't thought this his love of this holiday was going to spill over toward her, reminding her of great loss. Maybe, she thought, Ben had it right after all – maybe this kid, John, was going to be more of a problem than she'd expected. As quickly as she'd entertained that thought, Minna dismissed it. John was well worth knowing, no matter what challenges he might present.

Passing one another in the hallway late one evening, John stopped and Minna did too, placing them within two feet of one another.

"You'll join me as usual on Sunday for brunch, right?" he asked.

Minna smiled. "Well, I can't see any reason why not. Although I have to tell you, John, you're not doing my waistline any favors. You're a very adept cook."

John laughed. "It's pretty simple and healthy stuff," he said.

"I'm not so sure about your cinnamon buns, but I'll take your word for the rest of it. Oh, I bought a ton of grapes this morning. They're in the hydrator – help yourself."

"Thanks," he said with a quick smile and a warm hug.

Minna loved John's spontaneous, easy manner of showing affection. In the two months of knowing him, he'd almost convinced her to dare loving again. No one else had come close. Could she bring Gregory and Henry back through denial? No. Was she denying their existence by welcoming someone like John into her life? And what would happen when John finished classes at the university and went away? What if one more loss simply destroyed her?

On Sunday morning, Minna opened her eyes and smiled. There were snowflakes clinging to her window, sunlight painting each original design a glistening gold. And she could smell John's coffee, and cinnamon. She hoped he'd made those delicious cinnamon rolls again, his home-made version, not the ones in the pop-out can, good as they were.

Minna dressed in gray flannel slacks and a dark green sweater. With flat dark gray shoes on her feet, she walked out of her room and started down the hall.

"Minna," John said as he opened the doors to his rooms, "everything's ready. I hope you're hungry," he said with a big smile.

Minna turned toward his rooms. "You know, you don't have to do this every Sunday, John. I worry that you sacrifice time with friends your own age to prepare these weekly feasts."

"Not at all," John said as he stepped aside and beckoned for her to enter. "I love our time together, Minna. Are you okay with this? I mean, I wouldn't want you giving up something you'd rather be doing."

"Well," she said, "I suppose I could use this time for dusting or some such absurd activity, but I'm kind of liking the fuzzy gray look on my table-tops."

John laughed. "I haven't noticed a thing out of place or dusty in this house. Come on, we'll have a Mimosa to start."

Minna looked at John, then at the four-foot high Christmas tree. She stopped as if she'd seen a ghost.

"Are you all right?" John asked, alarmed at the expression on his friend's face.

Minna regained her composure, closed her eyes for a moment, then looked at her young host.

"I can't, John. I forgot that this was Christmas. I can see that you went to a lot of fuss, but I can't stay. I'm sorry."

John slid his long hands into the pockets of his jeans. "It is Christmas," he said softly, "but it's also Sunday. We always do our brunch on Sunday."

"I can't," Minna said apologetically and turned to leave.

John looked as though he'd been punched in the stomach. He didn't seem to know what to do or say. The Mimosas were a special treat. He'd made his cinnamon rolls, scrambled eggs with chopped scallions and tomatoes, and the usual pot of tea for Minna and coffee for himself. He looked at the table filled with food. After blowing out a single candle at the table's center, he grabbed a jacket and went out into the falling snow for a walk.

Minna heard him leave. She sat in her kitchen where she stared into

71

a cup of cold tea. She felt sad for the past and sorry to have created this gap between John and herself. For the first time, Minna admitted that she loved this kid. She cried thinking of Gregory and what he might have been. It wouldn't have mattered if he'd chosen to pick up trash. She'd wanted him to be happy. How, she wondered, could she pay proper tribute to her son if she gave someone else room in her heart? She fretted for hours, accomplishing and eating nothing. Sometime after noon, she heard the front door open and close. She heard John's footsteps going slowly, not running as usual, up the stairs to his rooms.

Minna stood, took the full cup of tea to the sink, then looked out through her French door in the kitchen at new fallen snow. It had stopped. It was beautiful.

At four o'clock, just as daylight would bid farewell to another Christmas day, Minna walked up the stairway quietly and listened at John's door. There was silence. She walked on and stopped at the door to her son's untouched room. She turned the knob and stepped inside. Except for the woman who came to clean every week, no one had been in that space for twenty-five years. Minna's eyes scanned the neatly made double bed wearing a patchwork quilt in shades of brown. Gregory had loved crashing there after an exam at the university. Her eyes went to the mirror over his dresser where he'd tucked photos of his friends around the edges, and she smiled at the old teddy bear he wasn't too proud to leave sitting in a small wicker chair. Minna looked at everything for the first time in decades. She did not cry.

After backing out of Gregory's room, she started to close the door then decided to leave it ajar. "Come and join us," she whispered to the spirit of her child. Then she walked to John's door and knocked. There was no response. She knocked again. This time, John opened the door. They stood looking at one another for a full minute before Minna murmured, "I'm sorry."

John's eyes filled with tears and, before they could fall, he used the back of his hand to smear them away.

Minna could see from the doorway an untouched table. The glasses with Mimosa still filled. The eggs, rolls, tea, and coffee in place. Only the candle had changed from a glimmering light to cold and still.

"I think we should take these things down to the kitchen," she beckoned to the thoughtfully arranged table. "We should probably let the eggs go, but those delicious rolls are still okay. And, I'm sure

72

there's nothing wrong with those Mimosas."

John looked down at his worn sneakers, then up to Minna's face. "You want us to eat the rolls and drink the Mimosas?"

Minna wasn't sure she could say what she hoped to, but she was determined to try. She looked him square in the eyes and said, "I made us dinner."

John smiled out of sheer surprise. "You made us dinner?"

"I did."

"I thought," he said, "that you didn't cook."

"I don't, but I did. I even made stuffing with cranberries and apples, just the way I used to."

John stood looking at his friend.

"Will you come and have Christmas dinner with me, John? I was hoping you'd be hungry; I am. And I was hoping that for dessert, we could heat the cinnamon rolls and plop a bit of vanilla ice cream on top."

John looked out at the darkening skies from his window then asked, "Do you have a tree?"

Minna forced herself to stand erect with her hands behind her back. "I do not have a tree, but you do. If you'll have dinner with me, perhaps we could bring our warmed rolls and ice cream up here; unless you have other plans of course."

John moved toward the table and began to gather the food and dishes. Minna helped. In her cozy kitchen, they ate a hearty meal and drank their Mimosas. The center of the table was set with a few old glass ornaments and sprigs of balsam in a glass bowl. It was simple, serene, and perfect.

"I'm blown away with all this," John said as he dabbed his lips with a linen napkin. "It was the best dinner I've ever had."

Minna found herself feeling emotional. "Good," she said. "Let's heat those rolls in the microwave. I'll get a dish of ice cream for us, and we can take dessert and coffee up to your rooms."

"And your tea," John added.

"I'm having coffee with you," she said, and John didn't ask why.

When they ascended the stairs carrying their after-dinner treats, John opened his door and stepped aside for Minna to enter. She walked in and placed the ice cream and rolls on the table. John set a mug of coffee before Minna's chair and another before his own. As he lit the candle, Minna excused herself. "I'll be right back," she said.

John was left to wonder, what now? He smiled then took a sip of his hot coffee. Moments later, Minna returned and placed a small box on the table. It was wrapped in gold foil and tied with a large red bow. Neither of them commented on the small item. They ate dessert and chatted about John's studies.

"May I ask you a personal question?" Minna said, then added, "If it's more than you wish to divulge, I won't be offended."

John picked up his mug of coffee, almost as if it represented a shield. "Ask away," he said.

"It's obvious you love this holiday. Have you been in touch with your family?"

John placed his mug down. He looked at Minna and said, "*You're my family now.*"

Minna had no reply to that statement. She pushed the small package toward John.

"For me?" he asked.

"For you."

John opened the package, respecting the length of red ribbon and the gleaming paper. Opened, he lifted the top from the box. Inside, he found a gold watch. At first he looked at it, then he took it carefully from its bed of cream-colored satin.

"Before you put it on, there's an inscription on the back," Minna said.

John looked at her then turned the watch so that he could read the small lettering, *With Eternal Love.*

John did not try to stop the tears this time. They sat in silence for several minutes, John's eyes on the message, Minna's eyes on John's sweet face.

"Was this for Gregory?" he asked, his eyes now on hers.

"It was. Now it's for you."

John slipped the watch onto his left wrist. "I didn't get you anything," he said softly. "I was afraid I was pushing it just to have our brunch today."

"You, John, have given me the greatest gift I will ever receive. You've made me feel that, once again, I matter."

John's eyes were filled with tears as were Minna's.

"Now," she said with a composed tone, "shall we have another coffee or a fresh new Mimosa?"

# SIMPLE PLEASURES

Jill sat at the kitchen table, her right forefinger looped through the thin handle of her coffee cup. The contents looked unappealing, like old dishwater. She took the cup and saucer to the sink and watched the swirl of milky brown disappear down the drain. She moved her eyes from the sink to the window before her. *What a pretty day outside,* she thought, *and what an uninteresting day planned.*

It was just after eight. She'd watched Donnie lumber onto the school bus at seven-fifteen, and Kristin had made her exit at seven-twenty-five, catching a ride with two other teenagers Jill couldn't stand; obnoxious, fresh-mouthed brats, each one of them. They deserved one another.

She turned from the sink and looked at the kitchen. *Lord,* she thought, *I really hate all of this.* Life seemed to be a succession of meaningless tasks and almost zero communication. The kids had yes and no answers and little or no comments on anything, and Cliff taught math and science all day so was perfectly happy to come home to a good book after class preparations for the next day. They came in. They ate, messed up the place, went out, and did it all over again. And like some demented robot, she went about cleaning up and fixing meals so that the process which *she* seemed to instigate, went on. Never enough time for simple pleasures.

Jill took a damp paper towel and wiped the table clean, then pushed the four chairs in neatly. She moved the napkin holder and the salt and pepper shakers to the center of the red-checked place mat on the glossy wood surface, then stood back to see if it all looked straight. *When,* she asked herself, *did I become such a perfectionist?*

She fed Plato, her white cat, then folded a load of laundry. Next, she tackled giving the hallway a needed fresh coat of paint so that she could stencil a design at the top. A quick glance at her watch, two o'clock already. She ran the brushes from stenciling under warm water then sealed the paints. Wiping a smudge of green from her hand, she grabbed her car keys and headed for the door to pick Donnie up from school and get him to the orthodontist. Even though he was just twelve, he was a big kid, tall like his father. He was pretty good, not too "with it" at times, but at least not fresh-mouthed like his fifteen-year-old sister. Not yet.

"Ma," he began as he slid into the car at school, "you're late! Let's go!"

Some welcome.

"It's okay, Donnie. We've got plenty of time and Doctor Jay always keeps us waiting anyway."

"Come on, Ma, step on it!" he demanded with an anxious tone.

*Maybe,* she thought, *he's just embarrassed about being picked up in front of his school mates. He's never been concerned about being late for the dentist before.*

"Okay," she said as they maneuvered through school bus traffic. "We're on our way."

In the office parking lot, Donnie looked at his mother as she switched off the engine. "You comin' in or what?"

Jill sat back as he was halfway out of the car. "I think I'll let you go ahead in. I'll just stay out here and get some fresh air. Okay?"

Donnie looked at her and shrugged. She was acting weird today. He stepped away from the door, gave it a twelve-year-old slam, and disappeared into the small brick building for an adjustment to his braces.

Jill closed her eyes then opened them again to look at the wooded area before her. It was considered town forest land, thick with late spring foliage. *Boy,* she thought, *bet you could get lost in there. Must be loaded with all kinds of birds, a nice place for them to hide and be protected from storms and fuzzy old cats like Plato.*

She stared at the wall of green leaves, then opened the car door and stepped out. She walked a few feet then pushed at the flexible foliage until it parted, allowing her into a cool, semi-shadowed place, removed from the hustle and bustle of life. She walked, moving branches and brambles aside, looking up occasionally at the neon sun straining to touch the mossy floor beneath her sandal-clad feet. All sense of frustration abandoned, this was a new experience, engulfed in silence and secret beauty.

Jill sat down on a large, granite slab and listened. All she could hear was a blue jay warning others that a stranger was in their midst. "Let me stay," she pleaded softly, hoping the birds would understand. She was there as they were, because she *needed* to be.

The sun touched her left shoulder and felt warm, like a comforting hand. *I like this,* she thought, *I like it a lot.* Jill closed her eyes and leaned back against the irregular shaped ledge.

> *If a tear falls in the forest but no one is there to see,*
> *does it really matter?*

# STILL

I go to bed at night clutching my pillow, burying the right side of my face into its yielding softness – just the way I once rested against him, listening to every beat of his heart.

When I'd open my eyes to look at his wonderful face, most often he would be looking at me, and then his sweet smile would stretch his beautiful lips and his grasp would tighten. There had been no one magical before him, and no one could ever take his place.

***

"Kim?"

I heard the soft voice vying for my attention, but my eyes were on the computer screen – I'd just received an email from the speaker we'd hoped to book for our school's commencement.

"Kimmie?"

I turned from the screen to look at Allison. I'd always thought what a nice young girl she was. Blonde curls embraced her oval face and her large blue-green eyes seemed tuned in to life.

"Yes, Allie, what can I help you with?"

She smiled, seeming glad to have my attention. "That student who wants to transfer to the college in London, I can't find his paperwork. Do you have it by any chance?"

I stood and reached across the desk next to mine. "Here it is. Marian took the folder to check on his financial aid. When you're through with it, you can just leave it on top of my cabinet and I'll get it back to her. Look," I pointed to the computer screen, "we have an acceptance from the senator we invited to speak to the graduates."

"Wow," Allie said as she read the well-known politician's note. "He's 'happy and proud to be chosen for our graduates' – that's fantastic, Kimmie. You're so good at this."

Allison smiled and started to walk toward her own receptionist desk then turned around and looked at me. "Hey, a few of us are going to the grille tonight for burgers and a few drinks. Want to come?"

"Thanks, I can't," I said, no explanation, but the truth had been spoken – I couldn't.

Allison gave me a perplexed and sad look, as if she didn't know what else to say and knew not to beg.

I glanced at my calendar as Allison went back to her desk. I hated this date, two years exactly since the accident, but I wouldn't and couldn't survive if I admitted to its existence. I covered the calendar with papers I could have discarded.

I went back to work, thanking the senator for his acceptance and adding that a letter would arrive by mail giving him the details of time and transportation provided by the university. It was a good moment staring back at that screen; this politician was respected – he would touch the hearts and minds of the graduates.

"Kim?"

I turned to see my boss standing next to me.

"Oh, hi, Helen. The senator agreed to be our guest speaker at graduation." I smiled at her but did not see Helen's somber face show anything more than concern.

"I know what this day means to you," she said. "Can I help in any way? Would you like some company tonight for a drink or something?"

I pressed a couple of buttons on the computer and the screen went dark. Reaching into a side drawer of the desk for my purse, I looked up at her. "No, but thank you. I'm okay."

"You're sure?"

"Yes."

I walked out of the administration building and off campus until I found myself walking to our street, to our apartment, to our bed. I stood there and slipped out of my lightweight coat and shoes. I looked at his space and smiled as I unbuttoned my pale blue blouse and unzipped my navy-blue skirt. My underclothes were discarded as a soft jersey nightdress covered my body. I knelt on the bed and crawled toward his pillow — he was there waiting with that wonderful smile. I lay down carefully next to him, my left arm embracing the pillow, my face against its softness. "I'm home," I said, then closed my eyes as I pulled the pillow gently closer, molding it to me.

# DEEPLY FALLING

She sat on a bench in the September sun alongside a foot path and a twisting, shallow stream. She could clearly see the rocks just inches below the swirling water's surface where mallards seemed to simply drift by, until she noticed their little golden paddles moving skillfully through the flow toward the sea.

She looked to the brilliant blue sky and squinted from the brightness of the day, feeling apprehensive and somewhat sad. Where had her life gone? She was home for her high school reunion, the twenty-fifth.

She'd gone to college in New Hampshire, married, then moved to Arizona where the desert mocked her desire to live as she'd grown, by the ocean. Plymouth, dear Plymouth, how wonderful to be back.

Nate had been a New Hampshire boy, crazy about the mountains and eager to explore the Grand Canyon and northern Arizona's offerings. She didn't want to go, but she didn't want to deny Nate his dreams either, and then after two years of marriage, a baby was on the way. Farewell, sweet New England, she had cried into her pillow as Nate slept next to her, unaware of her doubts about leaving for a completely different life.

She looked to the arched stone bridge to her right, her eyes scanning the cave-like shadowy area next to her, the occasional passers-by walking overhead. She remembered Joe's writing. It was with luminous blue chalk and in a foot-high cursive style, he wrote in a space about twelve feet in length along the stream's stone edge, two words, Deeply Falling.

They were all together that day, eight of them, friends celebrating the end of their high school years and the adventure awaiting each of them. Laurie, the cute little blonde cheerleader who had claimed Joe for her own, laughed and danced close to the water, teasing Joe that he must surely be dyslexic for putting the word deeply first.

Savi remembered watching him, his thick, dark hair glistening in the sun as he worked. She'd longed for him and loved him since they were children, but other girls had staked their claim and Savi stood back, glad to have him in her life, even if only as a friend.

With his artful task completed, Joe stood and looked at Savi. "What do you think?" he asked. "I mean, is it straight and everything?"

Savi nodded, but again Laurie teased that it should have been written Falling Deeply rather than the reverse.

"No," Joe explained quietly to a few of them who listened, "you need to place the most important word first. Falling can be a startling, stumbling word, and followed by deeply, it could mean into a dark place of difficult escape." He further defined his thoughts by saying that deeply falling meant with your whole being, intentionally, to a softness. Laurie laughed and danced around again, close to the water's edge. Joe looked to where Savi sat on the slope of grass and smiled. She was his best friend and one who seemed to comprehend his poetic thoughts and murmurings.

She could see it all now as vividly as it had happened twenty-five years ago, that sweet expression from a boy she loved, certainly meant for another. Those periwinkle-blue chalk words lingered, imbedded in her mind and heart. It was all so unmanageable when Joe hinted that what he had written was not intended for Laurie. It was a perplexing relief for Savi, having been accepted to the college up north, away from there for at least a while. But then there was Nate, so charming, attentive to her, and she wanted the things in life he'd talked of: children, a nice home, a life filled with joy and contentment.

Savi and Nate were together for sixteen years when things began to change. They separated but stayed in Arizona for the sake of their son. Nate became ill, and she returned to the home she'd once shared with him to take care of him until he died.

With her son now in a Virginia college, she sat in Plymouth and knew that it was time to return. She would sell her home in Arizona and live with her mother until a new house could be found in Plymouth. But for this bright September day, Savi allowed her eyes to drink in the memories and the present beauty. She and Joe had kept in touch through emails regarding the reunion. He was meeting her there, at the arch of the bridge.

She knew about his life. He'd graduated from Norwich, spent six years in the Navy, then came back to the Boston area to pursue his career. Out celebrating his thirtieth birthday with friends, he'd met Kate. The accident ended everything. Kate died and Joe was left with a hip and leg severely damaged. She'd heard that he was lucky to be walking at all, but he did so with the help of a cane.

She looked at her watch. Knowing he should be there soon, she opened her book to read with her sunglasses on to give her eyes a rest from the glare.

After eight or nine pages of the novel, she sensed his nearness and looked up. He was there. Tall, his hair still thick and dark, he smiled. A silver-toned cane embraced his left wrist.

She felt her breath squeezed from her chest as she removed the sunglasses and met his dark eyes.

"Savi," he said as only he could, "you're as beautiful as ever."

# WATCHING

Cassie McClaren understood that sometimes she took unreasonable chances. When her parents moved to Florida from Massachusetts, leaving their house to their thirty-two-year-old daughter, Cassie couldn't have been happier. She loved that place; it was where, except for a tiny apartment in an exclusive all female college, she had always lived.

The rambling old house was stunning, positioned in a patch of woods where it sat on a narrow slice of land one acre in width and six acres deep before one reached the barbed wire fence of the county prison. She had joked with her parents at times, claiming that their land was the corridor to hell.

The cranky old man who lived across the street from Cassie's house kept his yard looking like something out of a magazine ad for grass seed. He was meticulous and often complained to Cassie while she was getting her mail about the wild front yard she had, covered in drooping, huge pines and unruly ivy. He didn't understand why anyone would live that way and he said so. You wouldn't know there was a house there if someone didn't tell you. Except that, at night, the soft lights from inside could be seen by the passersby, probably making some of them do a double take. Her reclusive parents had liked it that way, and so did Cassie. She thought often about Julie, her older sister, who had once declared that one day the two siblings would live there and make birdhouses to sell by the side of the road. *Julie. How awful to have lost her.*

Every night in the summer, just before dark, Cassie unwound from her day at work by taking a glass of iced tea out back. Occasionally it was a glass of red wine. As a cost analyst, she was responsible for more than twenty people, most of them older than she was, and she found the pressure tiring. Home at the end of the day, she stepped onto a small porch in need of painting, reminding herself daily that she should buy the gray paint and just do it. But the reminder went still as she walked to a nearly invisible path and then into a shady, wooded area about fifty

84

feet from the porch, where her father had long ago built a gazebo. Sitting in there with a relaxing beverage, Cassie took great pleasure being in this secluded place. No one but her family knew of it. She could enjoy the night sounds as she looked back toward her house and the lights on in every room. She lived hidden and took mild delight in walking away from the place, leaving the doors unlocked. What was there to be afraid of after all?

The fact that she was alone both pleased and displeased Cassie. At times lonely, she also treasured the solitude. She was brilliant, and while not beautiful, she was certainly interesting looking with her long pale hair and bright green eyes. She took pride in eating light, an apple and a tangerine and two of those cheap little salty cheese crackers with peanut butter inside for lunch as she walked the perimeter of Boston Common at a quick pace. Men looked at her. She had nice legs and a trim figure, but what she knew was that she didn't want to get caught up with just anybody. A man would have to be smart, very smart, and he would need a sense of humor, and one other thing: he needed to be attractive. Not like some Greek God, just pleasant, maybe someone with nice eyes and strong, gentle looking hands. Muscular, tattooed Dylan Blaine from the mail room was attractive, but she wasn't so sure about smart.

Returning to the office after lunch, she inconspicuously checked to see if the purse she'd left behind and visible would still be intact. It was one of those things she liked to do, tempt and tease, hoping deep inside that no one would ever stoop so low as to touch what belonged to her. She knew that there were dishonest, corrupt people in the world – the prison in back of her house was filled with them – but she wanted to believe that people were mostly good.

***

On a mid-July evening, Cassie received a telephone call from a male acquaintance who asked her out. She put him off. He was *a Beacon Hill Brat*, she thought, not her type. The tea she had poured for herself was now looking pale toward the top, the ice melting in the heat as she'd spent time on the phone. She gave it a stir, then, deciding that more ice would weaken it; she poured the contents into a cup and popped it into the microwave to heat. With the mug in her hands, she scowled at the phone and then walked outside to the gazebo where she sat down in a wicker chair that had once been reserved for her father's

85

ample body. It was comfortable, and now it was hers.

It made Cassie smile, remembering how her father had built this eight-sided structure on a sturdy platform, but he had neglected to screen it in. Sometimes the mosquitoes found her, and when they did she splashed a citrus aroma repellent on her skin. She kept it on hand in the gazebo next to her chair.

On this particular evening, sipping her hot tea, Cassie listened to the incessant, night-time bugs singing in unison: the call of a not-too-far-in-the-distance owl and the faint bark from a neighborhood dog. She closed her eyes and considered Dylan, the office flirt. Probably a few years her junior, she smiled thinking of him. He seemed so certain that his wink in her direction would make her day. He would never know that she could imagine him with his hands on her arms, his body close to hers, his lips on her lips. And she could fantasize about them lying exhausted in bed, naked except for twisted pink satin sheets and maybe one foot stuck out from the covers. She rested her head back against the wicker chair's soft cushion and squirmed just a bit, as if nestling into his arms. If Dylan ever were to ask her out, she'd be careful to resist the temptation.

Cassie opened her eyes abruptly when she heard a crunch of leaves and then a breaking of small, fallen branches. What, she wondered as she stared into impossibly muted darkness, would make that much noise going through the woods? The raccoons stepped around such things, not on them. Deer? And then the possibility of it being a human, the greatest threat of all, sent a chill through her body. Cassie looked at her house, the lights providing a welcoming beacon. Should she walk calmly to the back door? Should she run? She sat there and stared at the house when her eyes caught a movement at one of the windows. She looked with squinted eyes, wanting to believe she was wrong. But there it was again, that gray shadow moving across from in back of the screen, the bathroom window, and then the light went out. Cassie sat statue still, the tea spilling onto her long skirt. She rubbed carelessly at the spill but kept her eyes on the house. How could this be? How dare anyone walk into her space without an invitation? Maybe the light had just burned out. But the shadow, someone walked across in front of that window. Now, she wondered, were they watching her from their darkened post? And the noise in the woods; was someone there as well? Could there have been a break from the prison? A thief? A rapist? A murderer?

Cassie shivered and leaned forward carefully as she set the mug down on the octagon floor. She moved her eyes from the house to the huge beech tree next to the gazebo, the one from which her sister, Julie, had fallen and broken her neck at the age of nine. She'd died from those injuries three years later in the bed next to Cassie, who was eight at the time. The tree's branches were accommodatingly curved and low. Cassie had never wanted to even touch that tree, but now it occurred to her that going up into that mass of dark foliage might be the best thing to do. She didn't feel safe in the gazebo, and she didn't think she wanted to go back into her house, yet she wondered if someone might be watching her every move. She looked up at the tree with just enough moonlight for her to see that she could sit concealed about twenty feet off the ground. She could stay there until daylight if she had to, and then she could figure out how to get out of there and to some form of help, maybe the police. She stood slowly, looking around her field of darkness, hoping to see nothing out of order, and then another breaking of branches, louder, closer.

Cassie moved slowly toward the tree. She stood next to the three-foot-wide trunk and looked around, her heart beating rapidly. She turned to her right toward the gazebo, then reached up to a shoulder high branch and with effort and determination, hauled herself onto the first low limb, and then to the next and the next until she was settled against a V formation. She was out of sight enough to be safe. She could also see her house through the plush leaves, the lights aglow, except for that one in the bathroom.

Cassie sat there, her bare feet against the rough bark, tucking her flowing skirt around her legs. She looked up toward the clouded moon, then down toward the ground where her eyes caught the pale blue mug she'd abandoned in the center of the gazebo. Her heart beat faster. If someone saw that, would they start looking around? She shifted her body closer to the tree's trunk and was intent on not falling asleep. She sat there and breathed as quietly as she could.

When she opened her eyes hours later, daylight had begun to replace the dark. Cassie was startled to find herself in a tree, recalling the night before. She could not imagine having slept on that precarious perch as she looked down toward the gazebo and saw that the mug was now on one of the horizontal rails and the tea was gone. She moved her cramped legs then allowed her body to slither down, grabbing for hand holds on the way to the mossy area at the foot of the tree. She stood there for a moment looking around before walking to and stepping up onto the gazebo platform where she reached for the empty mug. And then she noticed irregular spots of red on the floor. Wounds from scaling a barbed wire fence? An injury sustained from a policeman's gun? A stabbing from some violent confrontation? Cassie looked toward the house and then toward the deeper woods, uncertain which way to go.

She stood there annoyed with her own foolish behavior. So many times her parents had warned her to be sure to lock up the house when she left, and to guard her purse with her license, credit cards, and cash. Now she didn't know what to do. Someone could be in the house waiting for her to walk in. Someone could be in the woods waiting for her to move toward them. She sat down slowly on the platform with closed eyes, her head in her hands; she wished that full daylight would hurry.

With the sharp snapping of yet another fallen branch nearby and the soft call of a Mockingbird, she opened her eyes, covered her mouth, and silently screamed.

# WARM WATER

It was early morning and the sun had been enthusiastic about laying pale gold over everything not shielded by shadow.

Robbie watched the black sedan back out of the driveway. Crossing the suburban road, he stood next to one of the eight-foot high hedges which embraced each side of the driveway; he knew that place. He knew that walking on that gray gravel would make a crunching sound beneath his sneakered feet. And he knew that it would take exactly fifty minutes to mow that plush green lawn – he'd done it at least a hundred times.

He rubbed his eyes and tugged at the brown belt on his lanky form, then tucked his thumbs into worn denim pockets. The faded blue shirt was open at his throat to collect a summer morning's lift of cool air.

When a car motor hummed before the bend as it neared the house, he stepped around and inside the hedge on the right until it passed. He then sat down on the grass, knowing that from the road he was invisible. No one was home, until now.

Legs crossed Indian style, he leaned his elbows on slim knees and raised his angular young face to the darkened windows of the ample yellow structure. It was a pretty house. Robbie stared up to the gable of the attic and a single window curved at the top with ornate white-trim. He knew that garret well. It was all natural wood in there – floors, ceiling, sides – where long forgotten framed photographs and other works of art leaned languidly against the walls. There was an old sofa parallel to one slanted space wearing a faded blue hydrangea-patterned slipcover. In the center of that room, there was a small square table and one straight chair. As a child, before the divorce, he would sit at that table sketching, stopping only to imagine that this darkened place, its only natural source of light from the gabled window, could one day be his home – his own refuge away from harsh words traded by two people he loved. Why couldn't they love one another? Why couldn't they at least not quarrel so much of the time?

When it had all been settled, he was just fifteen, and his father had taken him and moved thirty miles away. He had not known that the home he so loved belonged to his step-mother, Kim. In going, he missed the house where he'd lived for twelve years, and he missed Kim, the only mother he could recall.

Now it was two years later. It was expected that he would go to college in the fall, and one had been chosen. But it was June and thoughts of college could wait. Robbie had told his father that he would be back-packing on the Appalachian Trail with twin brothers who had actually gone to China with their family for two months.

He'd taken a bus twenty-six miles then walked the last four to the house. In the left pocket of his jeans, he had his license to drive a car and a comb. In his right pocket he had a credit card and ninety-six dollars and forty cents. Enough, he decided, to feed himself for a while.

He stood, looked to the road, and then walked slowly toward the rear of the house. He wondered if she'd left the key in the same place. She had.

He slipped the metal piece in the lock and felt the metallic invitation to enter. As he turned the knob, Robbie wondered about her prized African violets which had once belonged to her mother. She'd always said that only he knew how to care for them. His secret was warm water. Delivered slowly to the soil and roots of the plants, he'd reasoned that he would not want cold water poured on his *own* feet.

Not feeling so much an intruder, he stood in that familiar kitchen then turned to close the door. His eyes went to the large bay window and the round table where they'd all sat together at meals. The African violets were there on the deep sill, all sixteen of them, looking tired, only a few in bloom. Robbie walked to them and placed his right forefinger in the soil of one, and then another. They were too dry. From the faucet, he ran tepid, and then mildly warm water into a pot sitting empty on the stove. One by one, he gave each plant a drink, careful to keep the moisture away from the velvety leaves. Then he pulled and broke off dried and limp stems until the plants looked clean and cared for. He walked to the door and tossed the greens to the grass where their blending colors would go unnoticed, then closed the door and stood back to look at the violets.

He ran cold water and took a cup from the cupboard above the stove. He filled it and drank its contents in a few swallows, then washed, dried, and returned the cup to its shelf. He looked in the refrigerator and found half a loaf of oatmeal bread, her favorite, what looked like baked chicken in a covered dish, some salad greens, cottage cheese, and in the hydrator, five apples and a fair-sized cluster of red grapes. Would she miss an apple? Maybe. He was hungry and should, he thought, have brought something to eat. He hesitated, remembering how she always wanted to feed him. He took one slice of oatmeal bread from the wrapper and a handful of grapes. He sat down at the table eating, wishing that they all still lived there together where they often watched deer as they munched on some of their greenery. She didn't mind the deer; she liked the gentle, graceful way in which they moved. His father thought they were a nuisance and talked of ways to scare them away.

When he'd finished eating, he looked to make sure he'd left no crumbs. He pushed the chair in neatly, then wondered if it had been tucked in or left out at an angle the way she sometimes left it. He couldn't remember and that bothered him.

He thought about his step-mother's rabbit, Clive. Was he still in the office cage by the window where he could see outside? He walked from the kitchen to the next room. It seemed smaller than he'd remembered. His homework had been done there, with Clive by his side.

The large gray rabbit looked at him, and immediately Robbie walked to the cage and opened its door to pet the long-eared creature. Then he went back to the kitchen for a small handful of salad greens and a few grapes, which Clive devoured. He checked the water bottle on the side of the cage – it was low and warm. He took it to the kitchen, rinsed it out, and filled it with cold water. Then he tipped it upside down and allowed a believable level of water to remain.

After his renewed relationship with the soft and gentle rabbit, he walked further down the hallway to the staircase. He looked at everything; it was all exactly the same. He climbed the stairs one flight to the bedrooms and glanced briefly at his old room, still pale blue with an airplane theme on one wall and the ceiling. From there, he walked on to a door and the staircase to the attic. He climbed the stairs slowly, looking at and touching everything as he moved. There was an old wool blanket draped across a top rail, a basket filled with skeins of yarn in three different colors, and an assortment of bruised and broken umbrellas.

At the top of the staircase, he looked around. Nothing seemed to have been altered. He walked to the table and sat down at the one chair, his palms flat against the cool, smooth wood of the table's surface. He glanced at the sofa. It could easily serve as a bed.

***

She came home from her law office at six. In her kitchen, she dropped her purse and keys on the table, opened the refrigerator and took from there a pitcher of iced tea. She poured herself a tall glass of the amber liquid then sat down with it at the table to look over her mail. She hesitated, trying to recall having tucked the chair in that morning. She wasn't sure, maybe, but what did it matter anyway?

She glanced at a magazine then walked to the office where she kicked off her shoes and left two bills on her desk. She said hello to Clive, tapped on his cage, and looked to see that he had pellets and water. He was fine.

***

One early morning in mid-July as she drank her black coffee, she noticed the beautiful blooms on her African violets. The one with white flowers and purple edges was huge, and the plant with the vivid pink blooms was crowded with color and healthy-looking dark-green leaves. She smiled and touched two or three of the flowers, remembering how Robbie had coaxed those old plants to their full potential. She missed him; he'd always been a delightful kid, so sweet, so bright. She thought about the bitter divorce, all that disturbing turmoil. She wondered if she should have fought to see Robbie, but she hadn't wanted to make things any worse. She felt the soil of the plants nearest to her. It was damp. *Must be the humidity*, she decided.

A few days later, while going over a contract in her home office, she checked Clive's water and food. He looked fine, but was he not eating or drinking much these warm days? His pellets and water seemed untouched.

She walked to the kitchen and took an apple from the hydrator. She thought she'd bought more. She sliced one, taking a wedge to Clive and the rest with her as she stepped outside to the patio and a cool evening breeze.

***

From the cabinet where he'd always stored his pencils, paper, and even old and broken crayons from his childhood, Robbie took supplies to the table where he studied the trees outside and sketched their

92

crooked limbs against the stark sky.

He wrote an essay on the effects of divorce on children and another on the proper care of African violets. He wrote poetry about what is lost and found, and he wrote about long-eared rabbits and how they liked their heads and necks stroked, but not so much their spines.

From the window, he watched the birds darting to and from the eaves and the trees. He watched cars and people and dogs go by.

***

By mid-August, while making herself a peanut butter sandwich on toast to have with her grapes, she remembered how much Robbie had loved her homemade peanut butter cookies. She smiled and looked at her lush violets. They were outstanding.

When she came home from work that evening, she kicked off her shoes, loving the cool kitchen tile against bare feet. She made peanut butter cookies, enjoying the sweet aroma for the first time in two years.

Each batch cooled on a wire rack, then was placed in a tin can on the counter. She smiled and moved them to the window sill, next to the violets.

# THE RED CANOE

Over the years, some fairly peculiar things stick in our minds, things that impress us, teach us, form us. For me, one of those things was a blonde in a red canoe.

Her name was Christy White. She was sixteen and I was fourteen. Her parents owned the largest cottage on the lake, two wooded spaces down from my sister's cottage, which was rustic, cozy, and all I could ever wish for. That summer, I was there three days a week, babysitting a seven-year old nephew and a five-year old niece, while my sister worked with her husband. Christy was there for the entire summer.

I didn't like her. For one thing, everyone, even my sister and her husband, would stop what they were doing, like eating a meal at the large picture window overlooking the lake, and when one of them spotted her they would say, "There goes Christy." She paddled a red canoe, dipping the paddle into the still water's edge, side to side, without tilting the slender vessel even a tiny bit. Her short, boy-cut blonde hair, was like a neon light, so pale against the most perfect tan. I wish I could claim that she wasn't all that pretty, however, that would be an untruth. Christy was put together the way someone might assemble a beautiful doll. She was exquisitely proportioned, slim body, the right bumps in the right places, and she had long, toned, tanned limbs. Her eyes looked like pale blue glass and her lips begged to be covered with red lipstick, the color of her canoe.

When she walked, which wasn't all that frequently, she was always in bare feet. The movement of those feet was exactly the way she sliced that canoe through the water. Her foot began by being provocatively placed, heel down first, then a distinct rolling motion to the ball of her foot. She curled her toes up so that the red painted nails almost seemed not to touch the sand of the lake's shore. One after the other, a sensual left foot copied the right until she reached her brief destination. And then there were her clothes. I never saw Christy in anything but short shorts and a sleeveless top. One article

94

of clothing was always white, usually the shorts. And she drove a jeep, no doors, no roof, which was also white. Maybe since White was her last name, she made it her signature color.

Everything that Christy did, people of all ages stopped what they were doing to watch her. The road behind our cottages was a sandy, rough passage. In her white jeep, Christy looked straight ahead, never acknowledging anyone nearby, tipping and hopping over ruts and roots as she drove. It seemed to me that her entire life was a staged play, each move so precise that it had to be scripted.

At fourteen, I had long brown hair and freckles over the bridge of my nose. I was unremarkable in looks, but I was never upset by being ordinary. I loved books, drawing, and writing mysteries. I didn't think a whole lot about wishing to be prettier and make-up was not anything I even cared to try. Not then. Later, a bit, but not at fourteen.

One afternoon as my nephew and niece played at the water's edge, I sat on the dock with sunglasses to fight the glare and immersed myself in a good book. I didn't hear her coming; she really had that canoe paddling down pat. "Hey," she called to me. I looked up and took off the sunglasses, squinting against the brightness of midday. That must have screwed up my face like a wrinkled prune, because she kind of chuckled softly.

"You new here?" she asked.

"I've been here a lot, but I stay inside sometimes with my nephew and niece. They like me to color with them and draw pictures."

"So," she began as she paddled her canoe close to the dock, "you're an artist?" She put a heavy French accent on the word artist, and it was evident that she was mocking me just a bit. She didn't ask my name, and I think she assumed I knew hers.

"I like to draw," I replied. I wouldn't have called myself an artist, but I could pencil sketch a pretty good likeness of my nephew and niece.

"Well, maybe I'll see you again sometime," she said as she maneuvered the canoe away from the dock, while I was thinking, I hope not.

Two days later I was sitting at the water's edge, talking to a couple of my friends who had traveled forty miles down to see me from home. One of them was a quiet seventeen-year-old, the other was his fourteen-year-old brother, who seemed to think I was interesting. I couldn't figure it out because he was extremely popular in his school in the next town to me, and he was undeniably handsome, a Steve McQueen look-a-like. All the girls liked him, and his older brother wasn't bad either. Christy appeared as she had done just days before, ghost-like in her quiet well-steered canoe. "Hey," she greeted us, then directed her gaze to me as if we were fast friends. "I was thinking that maybe someday you might like to go into town with me in my jeep."

I don't know if my mouth was wide open or what. Her invitation came out of the blue and had no reason behind it. Then she looked at my friends, eyeing them each from head to toe. "Aren't you going to introduce us?" she asked with a smile, revealing pure white and even teeth.

I was slow to comply, but then I did make the introduction. "Christy White, these are friends of mine from home, Mike and Buddy Crane." There, I'd done it; now these two could be smitten like everyone else.

Buddy was fourteen like me, but he was as tall as his brother and had a mature demeanor. "Do people call you Chris?" he asked.

"No," she replied. "People call me Christy, because that's my name."

I could see that Buddy was taken aback, but he smiled slightly. His brother shifted his feet in the sand, not anxious to tangle with this one. She looked them over again, then said to me, "Well, think about a trip into town. See ya." She paddled away, all of us on shore silent, watching her go, just as she'd planned. I was pleased when it appeared that my love interest wasn't interested in Christy, and neither did his brother seem to be. When either of them liked my girlfriends at home, they weren't shy about asking me for their phone numbers. Even Buddy, who tested and tasted a long list of girls, each time returned to me. He was incredible, but I was sensible enough to know that I didn't need a playboy; I wanted stability, someone to count on, and not at fourteen anyway.

*** 

I saw Christy all that summer. She stopped to chat briefly some days, and other times, she paddled by as if I were a pebble on the sand. My sister told me that Christy was an only child, her father a doctor, her mother an interior designer. I saw them infrequently; it seemed Christy was pretty much on her own at the lake, and she never had a friend down that I could see.

It's been decades, but the memory of her and that red canoe have stayed with me, surfacing from time to time when I think of the cottage on the lake. I have no idea what became of her; my sister and her husband sold the cottage eventually and bought a thirty-eight-foot yacht instead.

They weren't all blondes and they didn't all have a red canoe, but they were out there, like fresh meat lures to a school of sharks. She taught me the first lesson in realizing that I could lose easily to someone like her, but I also knew that what I could lose, I didn't need. Christy never again asked me to go into town with her. I understood, I think, from the beginning, that it was an ingenuous offer made to impress my good-looking pair of friends from home. Had she offered again, I would have declined out of the pure fear that she'd take me into town and leave me stranded there. Christy White was many things, but one of them wasn't that she was predictably warm and friendly. I knew I could never compete with her physically, and it never occurred to me to try.

Funny what a good lesson in life another person can be. Strange thing is, my husband, daughter, and I live on a river, and we own a red canoe. I didn't plan it that way. It sits out among the trees, upside down, most of the time. We only use it to rescue injured ducks or geese, which isn't often, thank goodness, because unlike Christy, we tip and gasp at every turn. I'm sure she'd find us amusing. She really was a smoothie.

# THE DARK HOUSE

When he walked past me on his way to the door, I noticed that the manufacturer's tag at the neckline of his crisp blue shirt was sticking straight up. I could have told him, but I didn't. The tag, to me, was a sign of imperfection, and Robert was far from perfect. *What happened,* I wondered, *to the love I used to feel for and from him? Could I place the blame on drinking and then the affairs? Could I place the blame on me?* Despite the darkness, I watched through the curtained window as he moved into his car. I hadn't changed; Robert had, so much.

After I'd listened to his car engine start and then heard him drive out of our circular gravel driveway, I walked into the room he used as his home office and turned out the light on his desk. I switched off the computer too, leaving the room in darkness, and then I closed the door.

In the kitchen, I lifted the top from the tea canister and moved a handful of assorted tea bags aside until I felt the small bottle. With a glass of cool water from the tap, I swallowed a pain pill. My ribs hurt, my arm hurt, and my knees throbbed. It was all my secret, the dreaded C-word: bone cancer they told me, and I really didn't care. No chemo for me.

I walked into the living room and sat down on the sofa with the remote control in my hands. I pressed mute and watched lips and people moving around on the screen. I didn't want to hear them: I just wanted my eyes to have something to do because they didn't want to close for sleep.

Through the French doors I watched a beam of light from Ben Crawford's flashlight, walking his dog as usual. I remembered my own dog, how I loved him and he loved me. He grew old too soon. And then I smiled recalling how a year ago, Ben stopped to chat with me when I was outside watering my roses.

"You know," he said, "I love walking by your house at night. All those pretty lights through your windows; I always walk slowly so that I can enjoy it all."

I'd felt genuinely surprised. I'd had similar comments from others, but Ben Crawford was not a man who anyone might guess would appreciate something like a pretty house.

There was one lamp lit next to me as I sat and I thought about turning it off, but then I thought of Ben and left it on.

When the pill began to kick in, I stood and walked to see where Sadie was. She was so thin, but at nineteen, I knew what pet companions know, nineteen is pretty old for even the healthiest of cats. I found her sleeping soundly; she hadn't heard me at the doorway to my sewing room where she'd claimed a soft old armchair that had belonged to my mother. I watched her breathe, then I walked back into the living room where I sat down again on the sofa and watched as silent people moved around on that bright rectangular form. I fell asleep.

When I opened my eyes, I felt groggy from the pill and cold. The TV was on, it was still dark outside, and the clock on the mantle told me that it was just after four in the morning. I stretched and felt stiff. At the age of forty-seven, I didn't think it was right to feel stiff. It wasn't right to have cancer either.

I stood and walked to the sewing room to check again on Sadie. She was curled up there, her breathing slow and steady. Then I looked outside to the driveway. He was still gone, not unusual for Robert these days. I thought about going to bed, but what was the sense at that time of morning? I went back to the sofa and pulled an afghan over myself and watched the muted eye opener news. I fell asleep around seven and when I woke up at nine, I got up to see if his car was back yet. It wasn't, which meant he'd gone directly to the office from wherever he'd been.

I went back to check on Sadie, obsessed with watching out for her well-being. She wasn't there, and I frantically walked around the house calling to her even though I knew she could no longer hear my voice. I'd wondered if she thought I'd stopped talking to her. I found her in the kitchen, looking hopeful over a bowl of water and an empty food dish. I fed her, patted her gently, then made myself a cup of tea. I counted the pills. Sixty-seven.

At the same time that my tea was ready, Sadie had consumed all she wanted of her food and had moved back into her favorite chair. I smiled, glad that she was still with me. *Don't leave me, Sadie,* I thought and begged. Cancer, loneliness, what terrible diseases.

I took my tea into the living room and sat down, clicking the remote

99

so that there was sound. I listened to babble for about twenty minutes then shut the TV off and walked to the kitchen where I left my cup. From there I went into my sewing room and made final adjustments to the design for Amy Wenham's wedding gown. Wedding gowns, marriage, wow – so full of promise. I sighed and sketched.

At five-thirty in the afternoon, I heard Robert entering the house. I'd roasted chicken, potatoes, and green beans; they were in the oven, ready to eat, but he didn't stay. He barely grunted something about a meeting to me, changed his clothes, and left, his cologne lingering in my space. At eleven, after I'd checked on Sadie, I decided to watch the news. There was a knock at the front door. My first thought was Ben Crawford walking his dog, but it was the police. Was I Mrs. Robert Harrison? Yes. They regretted to tell me, my husband had been in a fatal accident. I stumbled backwards. The two young officers steadied me. No, I'd be all right I said. They left and I walked upstairs to where he'd been sleeping for the past few years. I sat down on his bed and sobbed, not so much for him, but for the dreams that had died. All our plans, to have children, to rent a log cabin for a vacation in the Blue Ridge Mountains, to carve scary and funny-faced pumpkins for our front porch, all now replaced with whiskey and wry.

After a long while, I stood, smoothed the dark blue coverlet, and walked to the small light at his window. I shut it off and left the room, closing the door. Then I went to see if Sadie was still okay. She was. I went back into the living room and sat down on the sofa across from his chair.

My ribs hurt, my neck hurt, my arm and knees hurt. I stood and walked to my pills in the tea canister and took one out. Sixty-six left. I started to put the small bottle back among the tea bags, but why? There was only me now to know about the cancer. I swallowed the pill with tepid tap water then picked up the phone. I called a friend and asked her to help me choose a casket, no, maybe an urn. I made the arrangements for a casket to please his family after giving them the choice. It was a simple service offering sympathy and undeserved dignity. I didn't love him anymore, but I hadn't wanted him to know harm, and I would never have thought that Robert would die before me.

The day of the funeral, I took a pill, there were now sixty-two left. I checked on Sadie, fed her, then left with my friend for the funeral home and a day I thought would not have come. His parents were devastated.

His sister's eyes were swollen from crying. I felt sorry for them; he'd abandoned them years ago too, opting for a more exciting, secretive life than any of us could offer. My friend asked me to come to her home, have something to eat, spend a night or two. No, there was Sadie, I said, and I'd really just like to go home.

I walked into the house. It was dusk. Some of the lights weren't on yet and I left them that way. I looked for Sadie and found her sleeping. I took another pill, sixty-one remaining.

At eight that evening, the phone shrilled to wake me. It was my mother, checking to see if I was all right from two thousand miles away. She invited me to visit, but no, I said, there was Sadie. "She's just a cat, dear," she said, and I closed my eyes to her voice.

Two days later as I washed Sadie's dish and prepared to fill it with some deli chicken she liked, she walked into the kitchen, swatted at a catnip mouse, meowed softly, then fell to her side and died with my trembling hands stroking her, begging her not to go.

I wrapped her in a lightweight quilt and held her like a baby as I cried. After more than an hour, I took her to the chair in my sewing room. I pushed the button to the off position on the sewing machine's light and closed the drapes on both of the windows leaving Sadie in peace. I walked out of the room and took another of my pills. Sixty left.

I pulled a sweater on over my shoulders and walked from room to room. All my pretty little lights were out now. Ben Crawford would surely wonder how I was doing with Robert gone. No one understood that he'd been gone for a very long time before he died in that accident. We were good at concealment, the perfect house, the perfect couple.

The next day in a mix of sun and clouds, I took a shovel from the garden shed and dug a hole near to my roses in the back yard. I painted her name on a rock and wondered how I could bear to put her sweet little body into such a dark and forever place.

I walked into the house and went from one window to the other, pulling shades and drapes. I made certain that no lights were on anywhere.

Back in the kitchen, I poured myself a glass of Coke, and taking three or four at a time, I swallowed all sixty of my pills.

No more light.

# SHADES OF LONELY

Everything she touched seemed to fall apart; sometimes it did more than fall apart, it disintegrated.

What was the matter anyway? She was twenty-eight, stylish, self-supporting, owned a nice condo, had her Master's in Computer Science, and took an interest in life in general. What was she doing wrong?

With knees drawn up to her chin, she sat, drinking tea and petting the cat, looking straight ahead at the huge window which overlooked the lush green foliage. It was nice being on the fourth floor. You could forget that below your window it was just a parking lot with trees on the other side of the fence.

When the phone rang, she made a face and decided that it was either her mother or the office calling to say that the computer broke down again. She let it ring several times, vowing to get one of those answering machines she hated so much to find at the other end of her calls. When the persistence continued, she finally put her tea down and scooped up the cat as she walked to the phone.

"Yes?" She answered.

"Kerri? Is this Kerri Sullivan?"

She shifted the cat to her other shoulder. "Yes, who's this?"

"It's Dan Lombardi, Kerri. Remember me?"

She put the cat down on the floor and stared out at the gray sky. Why would she forget him? Did he think she had amnesia or what?

"Kerri? You there?"

"Sure."

"Well, how are you? What's new?"

"You called to ask what was new? I'm afraid you'll be disappointed to find out that *nothing's* new. I'm the same as I always was. How about you?"

"Not much has changed. Did you hear I got engaged?"

"Yes. That was, what, a year ago?"

"Yeah. Just about. So, nothing new, huh?"

"Not really." She answered as she looked around at her living space. It was all new. The cat was the same, but the place was new.

"I heard you have a nice new condo."

"How did you get my number anyway?" She'd requested it not be published.

"Oh. I asked the operator."

Kerri shifted her weight from her right leg to her left. She didn't think Dan had the brains to ask the operator for a number he couldn't find in a book. Now she was being nasty, just because he dumped her to become engaged to someone else.

"Kerri? Are you still there? You're awful quiet."

"I'm here."

"Can I come up and see you?"

"Why?"

"Oh hell, I don't know. Just for old times' sake, I guess. I just feel like seeing you. How about it?"

"I don't think so."

The silence from Dan was a new experience. Kerri sat down on the rug. It was stupid to have put a large plant next to the telephone instead of a comfortable chair.

"Please," he finally said softly.

"No."

"Why not? Why can't I see you, Kerri?"

"Because if I was your fiancée, I wouldn't like it if you went to see another woman."

"Yeah." Silence again. "Listen, Kerri, things aren't working out like I thought they would. I really need to talk to you."

She moved the phone to her other ear.

"Kerri?"

"What do you want me to say, Dan?"

"Say I can come up and see you."

She closed her eyes for a moment. "No."

She could hear him sigh.

"Where are you anyway?" she asked.

"In my car on my cell, maybe a block away from your place. Can I come up?"

"No." Her words were negative, her heart raced and she told it to be quiet.

"Kerri, why not? Come on, please."

"No."

Silence again, for several minutes.

"Are you still there?" she asked.

"Yeah."

"I should get going, Dan."

"Kerri, don't. Please. I need to know you're there."

She looked up at the ceiling then out at the treetops again. It was getting dark outside.

"I don't know what to say to you, Dan."

"Say anything. Just talk to me. Ask me what's wrong with my engagement to Sandra."

"I don't care to know."

Silence again.

"This is crazy. You're sitting around in your car and we're not saying anything. I really need to get going, Dan."

"Please don't go," he begged in almost a whisper.

Kerri stood and walked to the other side of her large window, dragging the telephone cord with her. The cat was nibbling on a plant and she nudged him away from it.

"You still there?"

"I'm here."

"You won't let me come up, but will you meet me someplace for coffee or a drink?"

"No."

"Come on, Kerri. Can't you hear I'm begging you?"

She walked back across to the other side of the window again.

"Kerri?"

"Yes."

"I miss you."

Kerri smiled, but it was not a happy smile. "What's to miss?"

"I don't know. Everything. I just miss you, that's all."

He should have thought of that before. Before he stopped calling her and started dating Sandy, the office flirt. He made his bed, let him go.

"Kerri? You gonna hate me forever for picking up with Sandra?"

"No. I don't hate you at all." She lied. "Why should I hate you? Sandy was more your type, that's all."

"I don't think so."

Silence again. Kerri sat down on the rug where she'd been before. It was getting darker outside. The treetops were blending in with the sky.

"Kerri?"

"What?"

"I can't handle things with Sandra."

Did he think he could handle things with *her*? Did he think she was crazy enough to give him another chance?

"That's too bad."

"Yeah. Well, sometimes things don't work out. You know what I mean?"

Did she ever. "Yes, I know what you mean, Dan."

"Listen, Kerri, I really would love to see you. I'm so messed up, I need to be with you. I can't believe I ever let you go. I had to be crazy or something."

Silence. She moved the phone to her other ear, covered the mouthpiece and sighed.

"Kerri?"

"Yes?"

"Please give me a chance to make it all up to you."

Kerri closed her eyes against remembered pain. It was tempting. She glanced outside at the darkened sky, closed her eyes, then opened them again to face the large glass reflecting a dim light in her living room.

"Listen, Dan, I have another call."

"Oh, you have call-waiting or something?"

"Yes, I do, because of the office computers. You know how they are."

"Yeah."

"Hold on, Dan."

She covered the mouthpiece and just held the phone for a few seconds.

"Dan, I have to go now."

"The computers acting up?"

"Yes. Darn things, I hate them."

"Yeah. Okay. I'll be talking to you, Kerri."

"Bye, Dan."

The cat walked over to her and rubbed his head against her knee. It was totally dark outside now.

# THE LIGHT ACROSS THE RIVER

When I was thirty-six and a widow, my sister decided to find me a new man. I didn't want one. I had barely survived the year after losing Joe to a motorcycle accident. She insistently introduced me to Doug. She said he had everything: good looks, intelligence, money.

After a few months of Doug, I reached a point in our relationship where I wanted to shout out loud that we were not a good match. When I began to dread seeing him pull into my driveway, I decided to explain to him in the most tactful of ways, it was over.

It felt immensely lonely at times, but I found familiar comforts in carrying on with keeping the bird feeders full (Joe's once-upon-a-time task) and keeping a few tiny lights on around the house when darkness invited itself in.

Holding on to routine, every night before climbing into bed, I watched for an airplane visible through my large bay window. It was always at the same time, just after midnight. I couldn't tell if the plane was commercial or military, but I always said my own little prayer for the safety of the pilot and his passengers. I also imagined that since it was time-wise predictable, maybe it was carrying drugs to some secret place. I wondered night after night.

Weeks after Doug had ceased to call or spontaneously show up at my door, I glanced out into the darkness of the woods behind my house just as I sat down on the edge of my bed. I saw a light which both startled and puzzled me. How could there be a light in the middle of the forest across the river which was just three-hundred feet from my back door? It had to be a reflection on the windowpane from something inside my house. I scanned the bedroom. There was nothing. I walked to the window and cupped my hands over the sides of my eyes. The light was there, steady and distinct, but why? It was just woods. I was fastened there, mystified, staring at the light. People had asked if I wasn't nervous living alone in such a secluded place, but the woods and its inhabitants had not troubled me. This light, however, was spooky. Who was out there in that forest?

106

I slipped beneath the covers of my bed, eyes to the window. From that prone position on my right side I could no longer see the light. I went to sleep recalling that a few years earlier Joe and I had received a notice about a developer who wanted to build six giant houses in those woods. Did I have a reason why he should not? I went to the town's planning board meeting and contested the building. He would disturb endangered species, among them, a pair of American Bald Eagles. It was investigated and ended the building of homes for very rich people. The woods would stay intact. I remembered the stern look on the face of the developer. He was a tall, slim man in his late forties. Obviously frustrated, he combed through thick gray-speckled hair with his right hand as he stared me down in that town hall room. I won on behalf of the animals and the trees. I didn't care about his accusing eyes.

I thought little of the recent noise I'd heard of pounding nails and the occasional power saw. Probably a neighbor, and the way the sound carried on the water, it was hard to tell from which direction the sound traveled. I closed my eyes and decided not to worry about it. I was a worrier who had been told more than once that most of what I worried over would never happen. It was true.

Over the next week by ten each night, I found myself keeping watch as I sought out the light. Part of me wished it would just disappear, and part of me liked the sign of life. In daylight, I drove to the street which ran parallel to my own, the street where the developer would have had to cut in a road. There was no road, no sign of disturbance to the existing foliage. I sat in my car at the side of that road, puzzled. Back home, I thought about it all day then saw the light again as it grew dark. The light became my obsession.

The next morning was a warm June day. Before I turned my computer on to begin work, I traded light weight pajamas for a cotton skirt and t-shirt. I made coffee, drank it watching the woods and the river, then made my decision. I'd fallen in that river as a teen, my friend laughing hysterically as I soaked my new pink shorts and white blouse, certain that my mother was going to kill me. But I was going to try it again, crossing the summer-shallow river with bare feet on slippery rocks covered in layers of minerals and moss.

I drained my coffee cup and slipped my feet into canvas boat shoes then walked out of the house, locking the door behind me. I left the key beneath a potted geranium and made my way through the woods on a

107

path to the river. Browsing the fifty-foot width of green-brown water, I watched as a few Mallards paddled past. I scuffed the shoes off and picked them up, then slipped one foot into the water, finding that it wasn't cold as I'd suspected. It was cool, nice.

Carefully, I moved the other foot until I was standing in the river, the water up to my knees. I lifted the hem of my skirt and took care to step on the flattest of rocks, watching for the resident snapping turtles as I made my way to the opposite shore. On land again, I waited for a moment before looking back at the woods and path to my house. I'd never seen it from this vantage point and found it serenely appealing.

For several minutes, I questioned my sense in having come this far. What might I find up the rugged incline and into the thick array of oaks and pines, a thicket of thorn-covered foliage and land strewn with aged branches and an ample bed of leaves? It was a maze of tangled nature, all connected by twisted vines and unrestricted growth. The air smelled sweet with wild pink roses and hundreds of tiny white violets surrounded mounds of honey-suckle. I watched as bees and butterflies made their choices. It was enchanting. I moved my feet into the shoes, glad for their protection against a coarse forest floor.

Moving cautiously up the slope, I pushed slender branches out of my way until I reached the top of a gentle thirty-foot high hill. I was astounded to see the roof of a small house. Just as I did, a dog barked and, before I could respond, a Golden Lab came bounding in my direction. "Oh, crap," I may have mumbled aloud. "I'm about to be discovered."

I was motionless, hiding behind an oak, the Labrador sitting down, wagging his entire rear end as vigorously as he could while staring at me. "Go away," I hissed. "Leave me alone, go away!" The dog sat still for about one second before resuming his enthusiastic stance.

I began to think about what was going on. Where did this house come from? I wished the dog could tell me. A man called out, "Murphy, get back here. Get back here," he said. "Leave the squirrels alone." A house, a dog, a man. What was happening here?

After a few moments, the dog looked at me. Hearing his name called again, he stood then bounded off. I watched him go and slid from behind the tree. I stayed still for a few moments before I advanced forward. I could see that the house was more a cabin, made of rough-hewn logs. And was that a cat peering out of the window? Yes, a white cat, and to the side of the house, a sturdy pen perhaps twelve feet tall. Inside the pen, there was what looked to be a tree house, and in a corner, a small pool, black but the size of a child's pool, about four feet across and six or eight inches deep. I watched that pen, amazed when I saw one, then two raccoons emerge from the tree house. They scampered down to the ground on a ladder, picked up and ate peeled bananas and what looked like eggs in the shell. I backed up quickly, again behind a tree, as the man came into view.

There was no doubt: it was Charles Slayton, the developer, with that unmistakable thick hair and those broad shoulders. So what was going on? I lost my footing for just a moment, crunching against dry leaves and brittle twigs. I thought Charles Slayton looked my way then he reached down and grabbed his dog by the collar. The Lab, his eyes toward mine, his ears flicking, was aware of me. I held my breath. They hesitated then went into the cabin.

I backed away when I thought it was safe and made my way down the hill to the river. I slipped my shoes off then took care in crossing the smooth flowing water, elated to be back on the path home. *Close call* was all I could think. *Close call.*

The next day as I sipped hot coffee and stared at the river from my kitchen window, I wanted to go across that shallow stream and take another look at the secluded and secretive-looking world created in those woods. I had a ton of reports to do for work, but I couldn't resist. In canvas shoes, shorts, and a jersey, my hair uncombed, I made my way across the water and onto Charles Slayton's property. I wasn't happy with myself for admitting his ownership of that land, but, realistically, it was his.

I scrambled up the hill, pushing briars and budding branches aside. Near to the top I looked up and thought I might faint. The dog was sitting there looking as if he'd been expecting me. He didn't bark, but he whined softly as I told him to hush. He stood up and rushed toward me, knocking me on my back, proceeding to deliver a full-tongue kiss. I grimaced as I sat up wiping my mouth with a corner of my jersey. The dog ran a few feet, then turned to see if I was following. I moved toward him, watching for any sign of Slayton.

In the distance, about two or three-hundred feet away on the other side of the cabin, he was splitting wood. I noticed that he had a stock pile, neatly cut and stacked near the raccoon pen, and the small house had a chimney made of stone. I begged the dog to go. As much as I liked him, I called Murphy by name and told him to go away. He did not.

Standing in the shadow of a giant pine, I allowed my eyes to slowly survey the area. Very few trees had been disturbed to build this place. It was orderly and yet serene, a perfect hide-a-way.

I watched Charles Slayton as he mopped his brow with the back of his hand and glanced around. It was easy to see that he loved this place, and he was probably pretty annoyed with me for contesting his opportunity to build valuable homes there.

The raccoons peered out of their house, making little chirping sounds. The dog looked at them, then at me. Again I begged the dog to go. "Go see Charles," I said. As if he understood me, the dog pranced to his master and sat down, looking at me from across a cleared patch of land. When his master rubbed the dog's soft ears, Murphy seemed to forget about his perplexing visitor. I looked again at the appealing cabin then backed away toward the hill, the river, and home.

Grateful for a job where I was free to work independently, I spent all afternoon on reports. Every once in a while I thought about the intriguing place across the river. That night, I gazed at the singular light for a long while before I noticed the airplane, its light and the soft hum from its distant engines; again I wondered where it was going, this traveling star in the night. It had become as important to me as the sparrows in my trees — it was dependably there.

The next morning, I knew before I'd finished brushing my teeth that I was going across that river again. I made my way, finding it easier this time. When I reached the top of the hill with the cabin in sight, I sat down on a fallen limb, scooting a few ants away. When I looked up, the dog was there, his brown eyes fastened to my face. "Don't you bark," I half whispered. "Go away, Murphy. Go see Charles."

Murphy sat down, defiant. Then he extended his right paw to me.

"You want to shake hands, paws?" I asked.

Murphy waited with his paw in midair. I greeted him as he'd suggested and that seemed to please him. At that point, I told him once again to go, and this time he obeyed.

I sat there in the morning sunlight, loving the way the golden beams swirled their way around the trees and through the foliage, lush

110

with early summer's warmth. A cluster of lilac trees stood near where I hid. I closed my eyes for a moment and breathed in the sweet fragrance; I caressed the soft blooms and longed to break off a few boughs to take home. I wondered why I hadn't been paying attention to the beauty in my own yard. Joe had landscaped with natural touches, rocks here and there, a nice mix of perennials, and colorful annual plants. This haven in the woods had opened my eyes. It made me think of the obvious gifts, the trees, the birds, the flowers seeming in competition and yet in agreement with one another. And it made me remember Joe. I'd tried so hard to forget what I'd lost, and now I understood that was all wrong. Joe had lived. His life stood for something, and I'd been trying to let go of those memories.

Standing cautiously, I watched where I placed my feet. Without arousing a murmur from Murphy, I made my way back to the river and home. There, I skimmed my yard and knew I needed to weed the gardens. I reached down for a few clusters of violets and buttercups. Inside, they were offered tepid water in a simple glass jar. I placed it near my computer and started to work.

Forcing myself to resist the other side of the river, I allowed myself the pleasure of looking out to the night and seeing the light. I stayed away for a few days. When I went to Charles Slayton's property again, Murphy was waiting at the top of the hill. He cocked his head and looked at me as if he was asking where I'd been. "Be quiet," I whispered as I ruffled his ears. "No barking."

Moving closer to the cabin, I saw Charles in the distance. He was piling split wood into an ample red wheelbarrow. He turned and looked in my direction, then he saw Murphy and called to him. "Come over here, you. Where were you? Checking on the raccoons? They're not ready to go yet," he said. "Maybe in another few weeks. You know the routine, Murph. Take care of the orphans, and when they're ready, let them go. And we don't harass them when they're grown and free. Got that down?" Charles rubbed Murphy's chin before going back to his wood.

So, this was his little secret. He was taking care of young raccoons until they could take care of themselves. And he was living in a cabin he'd most likely built himself, with no sign of a road or a car. There was a generator perched on a concrete platform to the side of the cabin. No wires for electricity necessary. This was a very cool space.

Later that day, I returned home from grocery shopping and found a bouquet of lilacs at my door. A length of twine gathered the stems together. At first I grimaced thinking that these had to be from Doug. But no, this wasn't his style. Doug would send roses or lilies wrapped in shiny paper with a florist's card attached. The lilacs came with a small slip of folded paper tucked in the bouquet. I opened it and smiled. Maybe I hadn't escaped being noticed. The paper was not signed. It bore only the muddy paw print of a dog about the size of a Golden Lab.

# NIGHT TIME

She was barely six when her twenty-three-year-old brother died in a car accident. So ironic: he'd survived the worst of World War II, came home in one piece, and then they lost him. She lost him – the only one who had actually seemed to care about her, the youngest.

His future had looked bright, unlimited. He was an exemplary student at Boston University. The family was thrilled to have him back with them; he was the bonding agent. With merriment abounding, his favorite cookies constantly filled a glass jar with a lime green top. The oldest of six, the favorite of everyone, his death brought the end to a family that had been as perfect as any family could be.

Her policeman father, who usually had a fine sense of humor and had been playful with her when he came home from work, became quiet. Her nurse mother became as close to gone as could be imagined. Her older brothers and sisters became angry, sharp with her, sharper than they had been before John died. It was a big mess.

"Look, Jinx," her older sister said one hot summer day six or seven months later, "you need to stay out of the way. Get a drink from the hose; I'm not opening this door for you every time you think you're thirsty. Now go on. Go play or something."

Jinx wasn't her real name, but they called her that, often followed by laughter. Her real name was Catherine. Jinx went out into the hot sun, found the hose, and turned it on from the outside faucet. The water tasted of rubber and it burned her mouth. She looked up at the locked screen door then went to sit under the Weeping Willow. She wished she had one of her dolls, Betty or Bunny, from inside the house.

In the garage, in a flimsy cardboard box, she found her old pale green glass dishes and remembered the tea parties she'd had with her cat when they still lived in Connecticut. Toby. She sadly recalled when they had moved up to the Boston area; Jinx was just about four and a half. They were on the train when she saw one of her brothers with his

113

bowl of goldfish, the water sloshing around with the motion of the train. She tugged at her mother's arm. "Mommy, where's Toby?"

"He'll come later," her mother said. She told Jinx that each time she asked about him for more than a month, then she finally told her youngest child that Toby wasn't coming. After that, Jinx never believed anything her mother said again, never.

Jinx took the glass dishes, a few at a time, outside in the shade of the garage. She found mud, took a little more hot water from the hose, and made cupcakes, all the while thinking of Toby even though it had been two years since he'd been left behind. Surely he wondered where she went. And where did he now sleep at night?

Summer was so long. Jinx would have preferred to be in school, even though she didn't think she'd like school much. Her only friend in the neighborhood had gone away to their cottage on the beach; there was no one to play with. She was a child with an old heart. She was lonely, even though the word *lonely* wasn't in her vocabulary. She just felt it, for herself and for Toby.

"Catherine," her father said, "eat your dinner. And drink your milk. Come on now, be a good girl."

Jinx wasn't sure what eating a hot dinner on a hot night and drinking milk, which she hated, had to do with being a good girl. She wasn't trying to wear her father down, but she did, by sitting there long enough, staring at the food and huge glass of milk, for way too long. He finally took it all away.

"You're such a brat," her older sister said. "We shouldn't bother feeding you at all. We should just give your food to Laddie and let you go hungry."

Laddie was her brother's new dog and she liked him, but she still missed Toby. Jinx eased herself out of the chair, her little legs sticking to the wood surface, causing her skin to sting.

"Go on," her sixteen-year-old sister snipped. "Get out of my way."

Jinx moved slowly, afraid to irritate either one of her sisters. They were getting the meals and doing the cleaning up now, ever since John died. She disappeared into the darkened dining room, then into the hallway, then into the living room where she saw her father reading the newspaper. She watched him. She turned and walked upstairs as quietly as she could, passing her closest in age sibling, who was seven years her senior.

"Hey," he said, "better watch out in that dark bedroom of yours: the big bad wolf is gonna get'cha!" He made a growling sound to scare her.

After he'd gone downstairs, Jinx sat on her bed and tried to see things in the semi darkness. Quietly, she left her room and walked carefully down the stairs, hoping none of the steps would creak beneath her sandaled feet. She made her way to the front door and turned the knob, letting herself outside. It was dark; she could barely see the heavily leaved trees against the night sky. She walked to her swing which John had built for her. It hung from a large maple tree, two very long ropes knotted through the ends of a thick plank of comfortable wood. She loved the day that swing went up. It had been John's idea and task, but her father had helped by steadying the ladder as it leaned against a ten-inch diameter limb from which the magic could suspend. It had been hard to tell who did most of the work in the offering of this gift.

Jinx positioned herself on the swing, her little hands gripping the thick, rough rope. She pumped her legs until she flew so high she wondered if she could touch the stars.

She didn't measure time, but she counted with each movement forward on the swing: she could count to one hundred, and she did that, starting over with one each time while watching the moon drift higher into the sky.

Jinx looked at her house. It looked pretty with the yellow flow of light pouring from the windows. She could hear voices coming from inside; she couldn't tell what they were saying, but it didn't matter. They never talked to her anyway, unless someone was telling her what to do or what not to do.

She was startled when the front door opened and her brother called to Laddie. He'd been exploring the yard, but when called, he started to run past Jinx. He stopped, looked at her and cocked his head, then when he was called again, he ran and went into the house.

Jinx slid off the swing, certain that she would be called next, and that they would all be angry with her for being outside in the dark. She stood there, next to the wooden seat, her hands still gripping the ropes, when her world went darker. The front porch light went out. One by one, all the lights in the house went out. She heard only the sounds of night: the crickets, a distant owl.

Slowly she sat back on the swing and wondered where Toby was.

Made in the USA
Middletown, DE
22 August 2019